Granny nothing and the Rusty Key

Ewen pulled at Granny Nothing. Her face was hidden in a great cloud of pink candyfloss. Today she was wearing a wigwam and it looked like a herd of buffalo were in there with her.

"Granny, will you take us to the carnival?"

Granny Nothing grinned. Her face was covered in candyfloss. She looked like the pink-bearded lady. "Oh, I will indeed. I love carnivals. There's nothing more wonderfuler."

You see what I mean about trying to teach her English? "It's wonderful! Wonderful! Wonderful!" I yelled.

Granny Nothing gave me a shove. "I knew you'd agree with me, Steph. But don't get so excited."

You can never win with Granny Nothing!

Have you read the other books in this weird,
wonderful, wobbly series?

Granny Nothing
Granny Nothing and the Shrunken Head

Granny nothing and the Rusty Key

Catherine MacPhail
Illustrated by **Sarah Nayler**

SCHOLASTIC

Scholastic Children's Books,
Commonwealth House, 1-19 New Oxford Street,
London, WC1A 1NU, UK
a division of Scholastic Ltd
London ~ New York ~ Toronto ~ Sydney ~ Auckland
Mexico City ~ New Delhi ~ Hong Kong

First published by Scholastic Ltd, 2004

ISBN 0 439 96333 8

Typeset by M Rules
Printed and bound by Nørhaven Paperback A/S, Denmark

10 9 8 7 6 5 4 3 2 1

Gulp

Chapter One

"Would you look at that!"

Granny Nothing peered over next door's hedge. Presley was frantically digging a hole with one paw, while holding Nanny Sue down with the other. "He's trying to bury her again." Granny Nothing couldn't stop laughing. "He thinks she's a bone."

Ewen and I couldn't stop laughing either. Nanny Sue did look funny. Her skinny arms were flapping all over the place and she sounded as if she was almost hysterical with laughter. Either that or she was screaming in terror. It was hard to tell with Nanny Sue.

Granny Nothing decided for us. "Och, she seems to be enjoying herself." She turned back from the hedge and started brushing up the autumn leaves in our garden. "I must say, she's surprised me. She's always playing with Presley."

I was still looking over the hedge. Nanny Sue was trying to escape, crawling away quietly while Presley dug like mad. And not a moment too soon. Elvis suddenly appeared round the corner of the house, whooping and yelling and brandishing a plastic hatchet. I think he was planning to scalp her.

"Oh yes," I said. "It's just a laugh a minute for her over there."

I didn't feel the least bit sorry for Nanny Sue. She had made our lives miserable when she'd been our nanny. Now she worked for our new neighbours, the Singhs, looking after – if that's the right word – Elvis their son, and his dog, Presley.

Granny Nothing finished brushing and waddled back into the house. Thomas dangled from her neck. Wait a minute, she hasn't got a neck. Her head goes straight into her body. Well, Thomas was dangling from wherever her neck was supposed to be. Mind you, who knew where Thomas ended and she began? They were wearing matching outfits, all-in-one lime-green sleepsuits, buttoned up the front. Judging by the shape of Granny Nothing's backside, it looked as if the limes were in there with her. All that was showing was her head and her feet. "You've got to let the air get at your feet," she would say. If you ask me, air is the only thing that would *dare* to get at them.

"You're wearing a baby's sleepsuit?" I had said to her when she came down for breakfast that morning.

"It's not a sleepsuit, darlin'. It's a catsuit."

It was more like an elephant suit, in my opinion.

"Where does she get her outfits?" Ewen said.

I wondered about that too. She had arrived at our door one stormy night carrying just one old battered suitcase and yet she was always dressed up in strange and ridiculous outfits that seemed to come from nowhere. Just as she had. Everything about Granny Nothing was a mystery.

"Right, I'm off to do my toenails, Steph. Come along, Thomas my love."

I looked at Ewen. He stared at me.

"Your toenails?" I asked.

"Oh aye," she said. "I've always been attached to my feet. You take care of your feet and your feet will take care of you."

She held up one of her massive feet for our attention. It was covered with corns and warts, and it had a definite cheesy smell.

"I've always had lovely feet." She said it as if she believed it. "Neat and petite. That's my feet."

"Neat and petite? They're the biggest feet I have ever seen."

Ewen stared at me. "Yours are nearly as big, Steph."

"They are not!" I was ready to hit him.

Granny Nothing loved that. "That's us, Steph. Feet run in our family. You get your feet from your granny."

She went off humming, her and her feet.

"Did she say she was going to do her nails?" Ewen asked as soon as she'd closed the living room door.

"I take credit for any good habits she has acquired," I told him. "I'm trying to turn her into a granny we can be proud of. I've already stopped her licking her plate after dinner. And I'm going to teach her to speak English next." She has absolutely no clue about grammar. "Who knows, one day we might be able to take her to a parent-teacher meeting and not have her attack Baldy."

The last time she'd been at the school she had come out of the toilets with her dress tucked into her knickers. She'd walked about like that the whole evening. And it's very difficult to think about homework when someone's knickers are in full view. Especially Granny Nothing's knickers. No one dared to tell her, or laugh at her. Poor old Baldy, our headmaster, had eventually tried to prise her dress free when she wasn't looking. Big mistake. Granny Nothing had turned on him, and lifted him into the air.

"I know I'm irresistible, Baldy," she had roared at him. "But control yourself!"

She had stuffed him inside the stationery cupboard before someone had informed her what he had been trying to do. And had she been embarrassed? Had she heck! She just roared with laughter.

"Does my bum look big in this!" she had shouted,

then she added, "Let's face it, my bum looks big in everything."

That had been the last straw, and that night I had promised myself that I would turn her into a lady, a granny almost as elegant as my beautiful Granny Fielding, Mum's mum, if it killed me – or killed her.

"Are you sure she doesn't mean nails, as in hammer and nails?" Ewen was thinking of Dad's conservatory that he was building at the back of the house.

I dismissed Ewen's suggestion. "No. My lessons are working at last."

I was so pleased with myself I positively skipped to the front door as soon as the bell rang. Baldy stood on the threshold, shaking, and I wondered what on earth could have brought him to our house. He never came here of his own free will. He was too terrified of our granny.

"Hello, Stephanie dear. I've come to see Granny Nothing." Even mentioning her name made him shake all the more. "Is she in?"

"You want to see our granny?" Ewen and I said it at the same time. "How come?"

He pulled a sheet of paper out of his pocket. "I want her to sign this. I am trying to stop the carnival coming to town. It's too scary for children . . . and I know how your granny loves children. And they have captive animals too, locked in cages, and I know how she loves animals. And anyway, if she signs this petition, everybody else will. So I came to her first."

I was sure Granny Nothing would do nothing of the

kind. Hallowe'en was almost here, and Hallowe'en is the perfect time for a carnival to come to town. We were all looking forward to the rides and the stalls and the candyfloss and the hot dogs. But I didn't tell Baldy that. I looked at Ewen and winked. "Do come in. I'm sure my granny will be delighted to see you."

"She's in the living room," Ewen said.

"Doing her nails." I added that to let him know that she had some feminine qualities.

Baldy sounded impressed. "Really?"

I led him to the living room proudly. For once she wasn't going to embarrass me. By this time she would be resplendent in scarlet nail polish. I threw open the door.

If I could have fainted, I would have. I'm just not the type to faint. Ewen is. He went down like a pin in a bowling alley. Baldy let out a moan as if he was trying not to be sick.

Why is it, that just when I think I've discovered all her bad habits, she comes up with a new one?

I yelled at her. "When you said you were doing your nails, I thought you meant you were painting them. Not biting them!"

For there she was, on the sofa with her leg up on her knee and her big toe in her mouth. Beside her, Thomas was doing exactly the same thing. It was disgusting.

"Och, at least I'm biting my own. Not anybody elses."

With that, Granny Nothing bit right into the green-tinged nail on her big toe. There was a scrunching noise, then to make things worse she spat out the nail like an expert. It flew through the open window and right over next door's hedge. Nanny Sue was recovering on a bench, sipping a cocktail. The nail landed with a plop right into her pina colada. Nanny Sue was too exhausted to notice.

"She probably thinks it's one of them olive things," Granny Nothing said.

We watched in horror as Nanny Sue drank it down. This time Baldy fainted.

"Do you think it might poison her?" I asked hopefully.

Granny Nothing bellowed with laughter. "Well, it's an ill wind that doesn't have a happy ending," she said.

Chapter Two

On Saturday, the carnival came to town. Everyone was there to see the parade. Polly and her sisters, Todd Dangerfield (who was promising to turn over a new leaf and stop bullying) and Nanny Sue. She was there with Elvis and Presley. Mr and Mrs Singh were there too, looking ridiculous as usual in matching Elvis Presley outfits. What was it about Elvis Presley that turned these perfectly respectable people into gibbering idiots? They dressed like him and sang his songs constantly. (If singing is the right word for their wailing.) They even tried to talk with American accents. They were standing with Mrs Scoular, another of our neighbours, who was waving a little Union Jack flag for some reason. And Baldy too, he was there, shouting out angry protests from the back of the crowd.

Nobody listened to him.

And, of course, us. The McAllisters: Granny Nothing, Thomas, Ewen and me.

The parade was a magnificent spectacle.

Well, no, it wasn't. Actually, it was pretty pathetic.

The bare-back rider kept falling off her horse, and it was the skinniest looking creature I'd ever seen – the horse, not the rider.

Polly pulled the beard off the bearded lady. "Look! It isn't even real!" she shouted, and the bearded lady – or the beardless lady, as she was at this point – shouted back, "I just had a shave last week. It'll grow back!"

A funny little wizened man cycled along towing a trailer with a box on it which declared: INSIDE HERE IS THE MOST FEARSOME CREATURE KNOWN TO MAN.

"What is it?" Ewen asked him.

"Sydney the boa constrictor," the little man told him.

The most fearsome creature known to man, and he had called him Sydney?

Then he only made it worse by telling us. "I would let you have a peek at him, but he's a bit shy."

The fat lady couldn't hold a candle to Granny Nothing. Not that Granny Nothing thought so. "My goodness, if I was as fat as that poor soul I'd be on a diet before you could say *fresh cream doughnut.*"

The owner of the carnival was resplendent in a red jacket and jodhpurs and a top hat. I say resplendent, but I'm trying to be kind. He looked stupid. He was a tiny little thing who called himself "The Great Alfredo". His outfit was three sizes too big for him and you could hardly see his face under the top hat. He was carrying a banner which read:

COMING SOON: THE GREAT GORILLA
MORE TERRIFYING THAN KING KONG

The only act that looked even vaguely interesting was the float of Mystico the Mysterious. Now, he at least looked like a magician. He stood nearly two metres tall, with a cloak of gold wrapped around him. On his head he wore a turban of green silk with a long white feather. As he passed us he pulled a rabbit out of a hat.

Ewen was really impressed by that. "Did you see that, Steph? Now, that was magic!"

"Ewen, every magician pulls a rabbit out of a hat. Now, if he'd pulled a horse out of a hat, that would have been magic."

Suddenly, Mystico's float came to a halt. He seemed to focus his eyes straight on to mine. "You must come to my magical event and you will see all manner of strange and wonderful happenings. But they can only happen if you are there."

Then his float moved off past me.

Nanny Sue jumped in the air in her excitement. "Did you see that? He spoke just to me. He needs *me* at his magical event or it just won't happen."

Ewen nudged me. "She's so thick. It was me he was talking to."

I knew they were both thick. Hadn't it been *me* he was looking at? Unless of course he was cross-eyed, and then he could have been looking at all three of us at once.

Ewen pulled at Granny Nothing. Her face was hidden in a great cloud of pink candyfloss. Today she was wearing a wigwam and it looked like a herd of buffalo were in there with her.

"Granny, will you take us to the carnival?"

Granny Nothing grinned. Her face was covered in candyfloss. She looked like the pink-bearded lady. "Oh, I will indeed. I love carnivals. There's nothing more wonderfuler."

You see what I mean about trying to teach her English? "It's wonderful! Wonderful! Wonderful!" I yelled.

Granny Nothing gave me a shove. "I knew you'd agree with me, Steph. But don't get so excited."

You can never win with Granny Nothing!

Chapter Three

Dad was building his conservatory when we went home. Or his "conservative", as Granny Nothing kept calling it. If it was ever going to be finished, that is. He'd been building it for yonks. And actually, he wasn't building it, he was supervising. Granny Nothing was building it. That is, when she wasn't biting her toenails or taking us to parades. She was doing all the heavy work, and he was the "brains".

"You should be ashamed of yourself, Dad!" I had told

him "Letting your poor old mother lug bricks, and mix concrete."

"Listen, Steph, my mother can tear telephone books in half with her teeth. A little bit of brickwork's nothing to her."

However, he felt guilty enough to give us all money to go to the carnival for the grand opening.

That night, we sat on Granny Nothing's bed as she reminisced about her carnival days.

"Your carnival days?" I asked. I might have known she would have more tall tales to tell. "Are you trying to tell us you worked in a carnival?"

Ewen naturally believed everything she said. "What were you, Granny? The bare-back rider?"

That really made me laugh. I imagined some poor horse, splayed on the ground, embedded in the earth and Granny Nothing in a tutu balancing on its back.

"No, I wasn't the bare-back rider."

"The tightrope walker?" Ewen guessed again.

Ha! There wasn't a rope that could hold her.

She shook her head. Unfortunately, Thomas was sitting on it at the time and he fell off and straight into her lap.

"They shot you from a cannon?"

I had a sudden picture of Granny Nothing wedged in a cannon as they tried to fire her from it. Instead, the whole thing exploded along with half the audience.

"I'll not keep you guessing," she said finally. "I was the trapeze artist."

The trapeze artist!

"But there was a terrible accident that finished my career."

I could imagine what that "terrible accident" might have been. The trapeze collapsed, pulling down the big top, and flattening fifty per cent of the paying customers. I was sure I could remember reading about it.

"It's a tragic story . . . or it could have been if it hadn't been for me. You know, I just seem to have the knack for solving problems."

It never occurs to her that she's usually the one who creates them in the first place.

"There was this lion tamer called Georgio," she began.

I guessed what was coming. "And he fell madly in love with you?" According to Granny Nothing, everybody fell madly in love with her.

This time, however, I was wrong . . . well almost.

"No. Georgio didn't. But his lion did."

Now I had heard everything.

"Leonardo, he was called. Oh, he took such a shine to your old granny. And Georgio was that jealous! He hated me. He was nasty to your granny, and you know how easily hurt I am. But I could see that Leonardo yearned to be free. I told Georgio that and do you know what he said? 'Over my dead body,' he said." She slapped her knee. Thomas slapped his. "And Leonardo heard him say that and he decided, if his dead body was what it would take, so be it. And one night, it came to Georgio's big finale. There was a drum roll and the audience held their breath as Georgio put his head into Leonardo's mouth. Did it every night, but this night Leonardo just clamped his jaws shut and wouldn't let him go. So who stepped in and saved the day?" She looked at Thomas.

"Grrrranny!" he roared.

She beamed from wart to wart. "Aye, darlin', your granny. I stepped into the lion's cage and I whispered into Leonardo's ear. 'Let him go,' I said. Leonardo shook his head, and Georgio's body waved about like a wee rag doll. 'Don't eat him, Leonardo,' I pleaded. 'He'll only give you indigestion.' But even that didn't convince Leonardo. Then, suddenly, I knew the answer, the only thing that would make Leonardo open his gob and spit him out. I whispered to Georgio, hoping he could hear me inside Leonardo's mouth. 'He wants his freedom, Georgio,' I said. 'Promise Leonardo his freedom and he'll let you go.' Georgio said something at that point. I'm sure it was 'I'll promise him anything if he doesn't eat me', but I suppose it's hard to talk clearly from inside a lion's mouth. All I know is that as soon as he said that, he was free. That night we left the carnival, me and Leonardo. We crossed the continents together, heading for his homeland: Africa."

"How did you travel?" I asked sarcastically. "By train? Did you get a rail card?"

Sarcasm is lost on that woman. She looked at me. "Not at all, Stephanie. I could never have got a lion on a train. We hitchhiked." Then she carried on with her story. "Oh, what adventures we had on the way. And once we got there, I set him free. It was a sad parting. We both had tears in our eyes. But it had to be. 'You'll meet someone else,' I told Leonardo. And do you know . . . he did. The next time I saw him he'd met up with a nice wee lioness and now he's got a couple of cubs as well. He called one after me."

She was almost in tears at the memory. So was Ewen. My brother is definitely one sandwich short of a picnic.

"I go back every so often to see him . . . but he's better to be free. Nothing should be kept in a cage."

"That is a wonderful story," Ewen sniffed.

"It's exactly like the plot of an old film I saw once," I said.

Granny Nothing sighed. "Truth, Stephanie, is a lot more stranger and wonderfuler than fiction."

"Strange and wonderful!" I corrected.

"See," she said. "You and me are that alike, darlin'. You always agree with me!"

Chapter Four

Next day at school, Baldy gathered us all into the hall and lectured us on the wickedness of attending the carnival. "You should be ashamed of yourselves, gawping at a woman with hair growing out of her face." He could have been talking about Granny Nothing. "And a poor woman who is so fat she needs a crane to lift her." Yes . . . Granny Nothing again. "And someone who is so strong they can tear telephone books in half with their teeth."

It occurred to me then that we had all the wonders of

the carnival living in our house, all wrapped up in one wonderful package: Granny Nothing.

Baldy rattled on for about ten minutes. Finally, he yelled, "Right! Who's with me? Are we boycotting this carnival?"

As usual, nobody listened. We were all too busy talking about going to the carnival.

Everyone met at our house that night. Granny Nothing was taking all of the children to the carnival. Everybody's granny. The safest person you could go anywhere with. Every mother trusted her. That really annoyed Nanny Sue. She hovered outside the window with her notebook and pencil . . . or her *portfolio*, as she liked to call it. She was desperate to find out something evil about Granny Nothing.

"She's got a secret," Nanny Sue insisted. "And I'm going to find out what it is."

She'd told Elvis he was to be her spy in the enemy camp, watching Granny Nothing, taking notes, spending as much time as possible in our house. Of course, Elvis told us everything. He preferred Granny Nothing looking after him anyway.

There was a wonderful atmosphere at the carnival. Flags fluttered, music played, and the smell of hot dogs and doughnuts filled the air.

"Right, what do you want to try first?" Granny Nothing bellowed. "What about the helter-skelter! I love the helter-skelter."

She insisted on going first, just to make sure it was

safe. And she got stuck. She and Thomas were wedged at the top of the slide.

The Great Alfredo raced up the stairs to get her unstuck. He was getting panicky. He looked at the queue of people waiting to go on. "I'm losing money here!" he was yelling. He tried to shove her, first with his hands on her shoulders, and finally lying on his back and pushing with his feet. She wouldn't budge.

"Have you got a wee bit of butter handy?" Granny Nothing asked. "That would help me slide down."

They tied a rope to her ankles and tried to pull. Still she wouldn't budge.

"Anybody got any bright ideas?" she asked, scratching her head.

"Dynamite!" the Great Alfredo suggested. "I just don't have any."

"I've got it!" Granny said at last.

"Just don't give it to me," I moaned.

Granny Nothing started squirming and pulling at her coat. "If I can yank my skirt up I'll be able to slide down on my silk knickers."

It was amazing how quickly that queue disappeared. This was a sight no one wanted to see. The Great Alfredo, however, was trapped up there with her. He had no choice.

Suddenly, with a wild "Yahoo!" she was free. I'd like to report she went spinning down the slide all ladylike and elegant. The fact is she moved down in a series of spurts making some very funny noises. Thomas, clinging to her legs, thought it was another wild experience, like white-water rafting." Yahoo!" he yelled. "Again, Grrranny!"

We refused to let her, though there was very little chance since the helter-skelter was broken in half, so it was really only a helter now.

We led her away while Alfredo burst into floods of tears. "My beautiful helter-skelter!" he cried.

Then she caught sight of the big dipper. Well, maybe not quite the BIG dipper, more like its baby brother. I knew as soon as I saw the size of the seats that we were in big trouble, but as usual she insisted. "Och, Steph, you could get a double-decker bus into them seats."

What she didn't add was that she was bigger than a double-decker bus. The train of cars creaked and groaned its way to the top. Finally it could take no more. It lurched to a stop. Everyone was screaming. Far below I could make out Alfredo, sweating buckets. "Come down! Come down!" he was screaming. "You're going to break my big dipper!"

Granny Nothing obliged. She yelled and she wiggled and then with one of her wild cries she sent the train hurtling earthwards. Now everyone was screaming! *The brakes have gone*, I kept thinking as my life flashed before me. It had been a short life. It didn't take long.

It was Granny Nothing who stopped it. She stuck out one of her massive feet and used it as a brake. I smelt rubber burn. I saw smoke. And the train stopped.

"Granny Nothing saves the day!" she shouted, and everyone clapped as if she'd done something wonderful.

Couldn't they see it had been her fault in the first place!

In the crowd I could see Nanny Sue writing frantically. And as we stepped out of the car poor old Alfredo was hanging up the "Closed for Repairs" sign on his big dipper. Polly was already pulling at Granny Nothing's coat. "I want to see the snake charmer."

So did I. The most fearsome creature known to man: Sydney the boa constrictor.

"Do you think it might eat somebody?" Polly asked hopefully. Really, for someone who looks so sweet she has some strange ideas.

We all filed into the snake charmer's tent. *Well*, I thought, *she surely can't do much harm in here, can she?*

How wrong can you be?

Sylvo the snake charmer was sitting crosslegged on the stage blowing his flute when we went in, while a very fed-up cobra lay curled up, just staring at him.

"Rise, o Great One," Sylvo pleaded.

The Great One just stared at him.

"Pleassssse?" he begged.

He was losing his audience – literally. They were all filing out, muttering, "He's rubbish. He can't get his snakes to do anything."

It was getting really embarrassing.

"I feel sorry for him," I said to Granny Nothing.

"Aye," she said, "I've come across snakes like that in my day. You've just got to show them who's boss." Suddenly, she bellowed so loud the tent flapped as if there was a high wind blowing. "Right you!" she yelled at the Great One. "Do what you're told, pal, or snake pie will be on the menu tonight."

The Great One took one look at Granny Nothing and began to shake in its coils. It shot into the air, rigid with fright, and stood to attention.

"That's better," she said and she dunted Sylvo. "There. He's all yours."

The audience applauded wildly. Granny Nothing took a bow. "There ye are! Granny Nothing saves the day once again!"

But the day wasn't over yet.

Chapter Five

I have never seen a cobra look so happy as the Great One did as he was shut back in his basket. Actually, I've never seen a cobra at all, but this one seemed pretty happy to me.

Then Sylvo the snake charmer wheeled in Sydney, the most fearsome creature known to man. He was a dazzling display of orange and green and black, lying curled up on his box. He looked like a colourful scarf that someone had left in a heap. He also looked incredibly bored.

Sylvo cracked his whip. "Sydney has been known to swallow whole crocodiles. They are still alive inside him as he digests them . . . and it takes him a long, long time. The boa constrictor is a truly terrifying creature."

Sydney just yawned.

"Sydney has been known to snap fully grown human males in his jaws and make them disappear. No man is safe while Sydney is around."

Sydney yawned again.

The crowd grew restless.

"Why doesn't he do anything?" Polly complained. She was out for blood.

"This is rubbish!" Ewen agreed.

Just then Granny Nothing looked around. "Where's my boy?"

Thomas, who was always clinging to her neck or sitting on her head, was nowhere to be seen.

"Where's my boy!" she said again.

At that very moment Sydney, at last, did something. He burped.

The audience grew suddenly still. Granny Nothing stepped towards Sydney. Sydney spotted her. He tried to slither back but he wasn't quick enough for Granny Nothing. She grabbed him by the throat. (At least I think it was by the throat. It's hard to tell with a boa constrictor.) "If you've eaten my boy," she said, "I'll have my fist down your throat and your guts for my garters!"

"Madam! Please!" Sylvo began to protest. "You are a . . . madam, aren't you?" No one was ever sure with Granny Nothing. She grabbed him by the throat too.

"Where's my boy?" she demanded.

"Madam," Sylvo croaked, "you are manhandling the most fearsome creature known to man. I can't be responsible for what he might do to you."

Granny Nothing gazed deep into Sylvo's eyes. She didn't have to say a word. Everyone knew what that look meant. *Granny Nothing* was the most fearsome creature known to man.

Sylvo began to shake. "Cough him up, Sydney. Please."

Sydney's eyes were crossed. He was going blue in the face. I'm sure he was. He was the same colour as Sylvo. His eyes were crossed too. "Cough him up," he said again. I thought that would be a very wise move. If I knew Thomas he'd only make Sydney sick.

Just then a tiny figure crawled through the crowd. "Hey, Grrranny," he called out, in an accent Billy Connolly would have been proud of. Granny Nothing dropped Sylvo and Sydney at the same time. They both crumpled to the floor.

"Darlin'!" she shouted, scooping Thomas up like a mother gorilla. "Where have you been?"

I thought he deserved a good telling off for worrying us all like that, but of course all Granny Nothing could do was slobber all over him while he screamed with delight.

I could see several people turning green at the sight.

Meanwhile Sylvo was giving Sydney a cuddle. The most fearsome creature known to man still hadn't recovered fully.

"Madam!" Sylvo wheezed. "I think some sort of apology is in order."

Granny Nothing beamed at him. "So do I, Sylvo. Thank you very much. I accept."

And she swept out of his tent like a queen.

Outside, she couldn't stop kissing Thomas. "Oh my wee darlin', I thought I'd lost you."

To celebrate his return, she decided to take him for a candyfloss. "He's been through such an ordeal," she said. Personally, I thought it was Sydney who had been through the ordeal but he wasn't being taken for a candyfloss.

Right then I spotted the tent of Mystico the Mysterious. It seemed to stand on its own, a sinister purple against the pink autumn sky. I tugged at Ewen's sleeve. He looked too and his eyes flashed.

"We're going in to see the magician, Granny," I said.

But Thomas was desperate now to get his candyfloss and he started wailing.

"OK, I'll see you later then," she said. "But don't go anywhere else without me. I'll wait out here for you."

I took a deep breath and headed for the tent.

Chapter Six

Mystico's tent was dark and mysterious and smelt of incense and wood smoke and greasy hamburgers from the stall next door. Silk scarves of every colour were draped across the roof and down the walls. Azure blue, sunset gold, blood red. All of it added to the atmosphere of mystery, and in spite of myself, I was impressed – and it takes a lot to impress me!

I only hoped Mystico didn't spoil it and start pulling those daft rabbits out of his hat again.

Exotic music was playing softly as the crowd filled the

tent and I saw Nanny Sue right at the front, clutching her portfolio on Granny Nothing.

"He needs me to be here," she had said, but of course, it was really me he had been talking to.

Or had those black eyes hypnotized us? Was that why I was here? Why we were all here, crowded into his tent?

There was a sudden gasp as Mystico appeared in a puff of grey smoke. It would have been a very impressive entrance if he hadn't started coughing and couldn't stop until someone brought him a glass of water. That kind of spoiled the effect entirely. Mystico began pulling a long string of multicoloured handkerchiefs out of his cloak.

Once again, my stupid brother was completely taken in.

"Every magician does that," I kept telling him.

Mystico followed that by pouring water into a glass and then turning it upside down. The first time he tried it he almost drowned Ewen (not a tragedy in my opinion). It took him two more tries to get it right and though he was soaked to the skin, Ewen was impressed.

I wasn't. "If he doesn't do anything spectacular soon, I'm leaving."

Yet there was something about those eyes of his, boring into me, that made me want to stay. Mystico began to speak. And his voice too seemed to be hypnotizing me. It boomed out across the tent. "And now, ladies and gentlemen, can I have someone young and beautiful to assist me in my next trick?"

I had to hold Ewen back from jumping on to the stage.

Nanny Sue was waving her hands about frantically. "Pick me! Pick me!" she screamed.

Mystico tried to ignore her, but she was already clambering on to the stage. She was so eager to be his assistant, she dropped her portfolio. Even when I picked it up, she didn't notice.

NOTES ON GRANNY NOTHING

She took the children far too close to a fierce man-eating reptile.

(That would be Sydney the boa constrictor.)

She attacked a harmless family pet.

(That would be Sydney too.)

She's building something sinister in the back garden.

(That would be her "conservative".)

She is always accompanied by a strange smell.

(Well, I couldn't fault her on that one. The strange smell would be either Granny Nothing herself, or Thomas with a dirty nappy.)

Finally, Mystico could ignore her no longer. He took Nanny Sue's hand in his. "This beautiful young lady is going to assist me."

"Saw her in half!" I called out hopefully.

But actually he had an even better plan in mind. He was going to make her disappear. All the children were cheering wildly as he pushed a wooden cubicle on to the stage. A curtain of green silk was draped in front and Mystico drew it aside and stepped into the cubicle. He tapped the walls to let us see that there was no way out once Nanny Sue was inside the box.

"And what is the name of my beautiful assistant?"

Nanny Sue giggled like someone's whose brain had been removed. "Sue," she simpered.

Mystico turned back to his audience. "Let's give the lovely Stew a round of applause."

She tried to correct him, but he wasn't listening. The "lovely Stew" she remained. I thought it suited her. She always looked like a dog's dinner to me anyway.

He asked her to step inside the cubicle and he hauled the curtain closed dramatically. He tapped the walls three times and there was a puff of red smoke.

"Behold! The Magic of Mystico!" he cried and he pulled the curtain open.

The lovely Stew was still there. Looking *stew-pid*, I might add.

Mystico was annoyed but he covered it beautifully. He drew the curtain shut. He tapped the walls three times. "Once again," he cried, "the Magic of Mystico!"

This time a great cloud of green smoke filled the air. He hauled the curtain across with a flourish.

The lovely Stew was still there.

"Saw her in half!" I suggested again. Surely he could get that right?

But Mystico was determined not to give up. He stuck his head inside the cubicle and muttered something to Nanny Sue. I was sure it was, "It's not that hard, Stew.

There's a trap door under your feet. Are you completely thick!"

However, I might have been mistaken, for when he turned back to the audience he had a big grin on his face.

This time he was even more dramatic. He danced around the stage like a whirling dervish thing. There were clouds of green smoke and red smoke and blue smoke. Finally, he halted at the cubicle. Again he said the magic words, "the Magic of Mystico," and this time he stamped his feet really hard on the stage.

There was a shriek from inside the cubicle.

He must have done the trick, for when he pulled the curtain across this time, the lovely Stew had gone. The audience applauded. Well, just a little.

"Shall I bring the lovely Stew back?" Mystico asked.

"No!" everyone shouted.

Nanny Sue was not popular. However, it was too late. He pointed to the entrance of the tent and there she was. Her hair was standing on end and she looked as if she had been dragged through a hedge backwards, but she was beaming from ear to ear and bowing like a star.

"Ta-ra!" she shouted, dancing towards the stage.

"The lovely Stew has returned, thanks to the Magic of Mystico!"

Between you and me, I think he was already sorry. Nanny Sue leapt on to the stage and almost pushed him aside to take her bow. She was blowing kisses at the crowd. "This is what I was meant to be!" she said. "A star!"

Now Mystico pushed her aside. "And now for Mystico's Box of Mystery."

Almost as if it was being pushed by unseen hands, a box rolled towards the front of the stage. It was encrusted with pearls and emeralds and rubies and diamonds. It came to a halt right in front of me.

"I have just returned from a successful tour of the Caribbean. It was on the mysterious island of Martinique that I came across this Box. Worshipped and feared by the superstitious islanders, it was kept hidden deep in the island's many caves. What is inside the Box? No one knows. Could it be pirates' treasure? Could it be the secret of eternal youth? Only one key in all the world can open this Box. One key. Could yours be that key? Would you like to open the Box?"

He was talking directly to me, I was sure of it. "You must know what's inside it," I said.

"Magic," he said mysteriously. "And mystery. And whatever is inside it, you keep. And not only that. . ." He held up a wad of notes. "Whoever opens the Box can have all this too."

There was a stampede. Keys jangled everywhere. Yale keys, jail keys, mortice keys, chubb keys, long keys, short keys, car keys, door keys, safe keys, house keys.

But none of them opened the Box. It sat there, daring us to get inside and find out its secret.

I don't know what it was about that Box. It certainly wasn't the reward. I wasn't interested in that. But from that moment I knew I wouldn't be happy until I opened that Box and found out what was inside.

Chapter Seven

Granny Nothing was waiting for us when we got outside the tent. "Right! Is everybody here?" Then she counted us out. "Polly, Elvis, Presley, Todd, Ewen, Steph." She stared down at me. "Steph? Are you OK? You look as if you're in a daze."

"She's been like that since we saw Mystico," Ewen blabbed out. "I think he's hypnotized her."

"Oh, I know how to fix that." And with that she clapped her hands together. It was like thunder. Enough to waken the dead in the local cemetery. It certainly woke me up.

"Always works," Granny Nothing said. "So, where do you want to go next?"

Considering she'd broken the helter-skelter and the big dipper, there wasn't a lot left for us to go to.

Suddenly Polly was leaping about and screaming with excitement. "There! There! I want to go there!"

She was pointing at a tatty old tent with a lopsided sign which proclaimed: THE HALL OF MIRRORS.

"Let's go!" Granny Nothing yelled.

Granny Nothing in the hall of mirrors. I could guess what would happen next. One look from her and every one would crack.

We all filed in and made our way along a black tunnel of mirrors.

"Look at me. I'm so tall!" Polly shouted. And she was. The mirror made her look stick-thin, with a long swan-like neck and a face like a horse.

Elvis was giggling. "Look at us!"

Elvis and Presley were flat and squat, like two toads.

Ewen was screaming. His head had actually separated from his body. His neck had totally disappeared. A real improvement, in my opinion.

Baby Thomas crawled to his reflection and started kissing the baby monster in the mirror. "There's hardly any change there. He looks exactly the same," I pointed out.

"My boy's bootiful," Granny Nothing exclaimed, lifting him into her arms. "We're both bootiful."

Now two monsters grinned back from the mirror.

"Bootiful," Thomas agreed, in his deep Glaswegian accent.

There were mirrors that made us all look fat, and mirrors that made us all look thin. Mirrors that gave us tiny heads, and mirrors that gave us huge bodies. Mirrors that made us laugh, and mirrors that made us scream in horror.

Suddenly, Ewen grabbed my arm. Everyone gasped. We couldn't believe what we were seeing.

Granny Nothing had stopped in front of a mirror.

And Granny Nothing was . . . beautiful.

The image that stared back at her was slim with shapely legs and a perfect face. Gone were the warts, and the facial hair and the wrinkled-stocking legs. She even looked as if she had teeth. White ones.

We were all gobsmacked. Our gobs had never been so smacked.

Granny Nothing stared at her reflection. "Well, what do you think of that?" She sounded gobsmacked too.

"That's amazing!" Ewen said. And we all agreed. "Amazing!"

Granny Nothing looked around at us. "I'm going to ask for my money back. There's nothing wrong with this mirror. It's a perfectly ordinary mirror. I always look like that, don't I? Bootiful. In fact. . ." She turned to see her side view. "Look at that bum. It's a wee beauty. Forget the diet. I'm perfect as I am."

She moved on, a happy woman. Now I stepped in front of the mirror. It was the biggest mistake of my life.

"Stephanie! Look at you!"

I was staggered, stunned, horrified. I couldn't

breathe. I thought I was going to faint. I looked into the mirror and I was staring at. . .

Granny Nothing.

I looked exactly like her. From the warts on my face, right down to the legs that looked as if they were wearing wrinkled stockings.

"This can't be!" I screamed. "I don't look like this. I don't."

Ewen was delighted. "Steph, you're Granny Nothing's spitting image."

I think I was still screaming when we got home.

Chapter Eight

Once again Baldy was trying to convince us not to go back to the carnival.

"I can't believe you would gawk at a poor old woman with a beard."

"It wasn't a real beard," Polly pointed out. "I pulled it and it came off."

"It's growing in quite nicely now," Todd Dangerfield told her. "I pulled it yesterday and it was real. Was she mad!"

That made us all laugh. Especially since she'd sat on Todd for half and hour till he apologized.

Baldy's lip began to quiver. "Have you no finer feelings for your fellow human beings?"

"No," someone shouted. I think it might have been me.

"Well, what about the animals? Animals should not be kept in cages."

I tried to think what animals they had at the carnival. "They've only got a flea circus and a boa constrictor."

"And my granny strangled the boa constrictor because she thought he'd eaten Thomas," Ewen said proudly.

Mention of Granny Nothing made Baldy's legs quiver as well as his lip.

"Boa constrictors were not meant to be entertainment for the masses. They are wild and beautiful creatures who were meant to roam free."

"And crush people to death, then swallow them," Ewen said loudly.

Polly looked sick. "Swallow them whole?"

Ewen nodded. He'd been reading up on boa constrictors. Had a notion he too might become a snake charmer when he grew up. He'd been practising on worms in the garden. "Then they digest them. Slowly. It takes weeks and weeks."

"What do they feed them on at the carnival?"

That made everybody think. What did they feed Sidney on? I made a mental note that if anyone went missing, the boa would be the chief suspect.

Baldy realized he wasn't getting anywhere. He made one final attempt. "There is a magician who saws women in half. That is an insult to women everywhere."

"He'll saw men in half too," Ewen said. "And anyway, he's rubbish. He made Nanny Sue disappear and then he brought her back."

"Magic is evil. A bad influence. We must make a stand against this evil in our midst. Are you with me?"

By this time everyone had stopped listening to him. Polly had a box of Liquorice Allsorts and we were picking our favourites.

He shouted again, louder this time. "Are you with me?"

"No!" I shouted back and we all began to drift from the hall. Of course we were all going back to the carnival. There was nothing else to do in town. And anyway, it was so bad, it was fun. Besides that . . . there was Mystico. I couldn't stop thinking about him, and the box. Nothing would keep me from going back.

Baldy stamped his feet a few times and called out: "You are a bunch of unnatural children. Monsters, all of you! Right. Who needs you! I'll do it myself."

When we got home, Dad was still building his "conservative" or should I say, Granny Nothing was. She was hammering in the nails. Thomas was clinging on to her back. Dad was lying on the sofa having a cup of tea. He jumped when he saw us. "I just sat down this minute. I've been working hard. So I have, Mother?"

Granny Nothing stopped hammering for a moment and grinned. It looked as if she had a mouthful of steel teeth. A closer look told me she was firing the nails into the wood from her mouth. "The boy needed a wee rest," she said, and I realized that Dad was just as much her "boy" as Thomas was.

"I think you should be ashamed of yourself, Dad!" I said.

"I'm the brains of the team," he said, and he went back to his tea.

I spotted Nanny Sue's head peeping over the garden hedge. "How long has she been there?"

"She's been watching me erecting my conservative," Granny Nothing said. "Just ignore her."

Suddenly, there was a barking and a yelping and Nanny Sue's head began to bob wildly before it disappeared altogether. Clearly, Presley was trying to bury her again.

It was while I was doing my homework that there was a sudden pounding on our door.

"Who on earth is that?" Dad said, getting up to answer it.

Granny Nothing held him back. "I'll go, son. It might be a serial killer. Strange people come out of the woodwork when the clocks go back."

None stranger than Granny Nothing.

She thundered to the door and pulled it open.

It wasn't a serial killer. It was the Great Alfredo. His face was red, and he was almost in tears. "You! You did this to me!"

Granny Nothing lifted him by his shirt and glared at him. "That's no way to talk to a lady," she said.

"My helter-skelter can only helter, and my big dipper

can't dip. And now Sydney the boa constrictor's run away from the circus. All because of you."

Granny Nothing was all innocence. "Because of me? What did I do?"

"Attempted murder, that's what! And now Sylvo's run after him. I've lost my snake charmer as well."

The little carnival owner stood erect. His top hat fell down over his eyes. He pushed it back and looked up at Granny Nothing as she loomed over him like a black cloud. "Madam," he said, "you are ruining my livelihood. And I have come here to tell you that when my star attraction arrives, my gorilla, you had better not frighten him away. He is my last chance to make money." He turned on his heel and left, tripping up halfway down the path and falling flat on his face, which rather spoiled his dignified exit.

"What a cheek!" Granny Nothing said. "It was never attempted murder. Grievous bodily harm at the very most."

"Maybe you'd better not go back to that carnival," Dad suggested.

Ewen was having none of that. "No, Dad. It's Granny Nothing who takes us all to the carnival. If she doesn't go, we don't get to go either!"

Granny Nothing was so pleased with that she lifted Ewen by the shoulders and kissed him. Ewen was stunned. He hadn't expected that. "Thanks for that vote of confidence, son. Of course I'm going back. He was exaggerating. You know these showbiz people." Then she waddled into the kitchen to finish erecting her "conservative".

There was no way I wasn't going back to the carnival. I was looking forward to it. Because I had decided that we might just have a key which would open Mystico's Box of Mystery.

But first I had to steal it from Granny Nothing's suitcase.

Chapter Nine

"Where's her case now?" Ewen asked me when I told him my plan.

Granny Nothing had moved her famous suitcase from the cupboard at the top of the stairs to "somewhere safer", she said. I don't think she trusted us. Just because we had once stolen a shrunken head from it.

"That head's got sentimental value," she had said, sniffing back a tear. It had once been attached to her fiancé. Now, she kept the shrunken head under her bed and used it to crack walnuts. So romantic.

"The case is in the cellar," I told Ewen. "We'll go down while Granny Nothing's giving Thomas his bath, or licking him clean or whatever she does. Dad will be having a snooze after all his hard work."

Dad was really beginning to annoy me. Hard work, indeed, watching his mother do everything.

"And where will Mum be?"

"Mum will be at Mrs Singh's. They're making the costumes for Hallowe'en."

"I don't want to go down to the cellar, Steph. It's dark down there."

"I'll put the light on . . . but it won't suit me." My joke was lost on Ewen.

"Couldn't you just go down and get the key yourself?"

"No, I could not. We're a team you and me. Why? Are you scared? Are you a man or a mouse, Ewen McAllister?"

"Throw me a bit of cheese and you'll soon find out."

"You're coming with me, and that's all there is to it."

"You really are brave, Steph. You're never scared."

I clutched tight on to Ewen's hand as we began to creep down the cellar steps. We could hear Granny Nothing's shouts of protest ringing out through the house. She didn't approve of baths. "If the Good Lord had meant us to have baths, he would have made us all fish."

And she would have been a whale.

Every so often we could hear Thomas let out a wild cry of agreement. He hated baths too.

Even with the light switched on the cellar was dark. One dim bulb swung backwards and forwards, sending eerie shadows dancing all around the walls. Ewen moved closer. "Let's get the key and get out of here."

The problem was, where exactly was the case, and how were we going to find it among all the junk down here? There were things I hadn't seen in years. Dad's rowing machine: hardly used. Mum's exercise bike: hardly used. An old computer, my old pram, Ewen's rocking horse and a couple of easy chairs that had seen better days, stacks of boxes and black bin-bags.

"We'll never find it," Ewen whispered. "Let's just go back up."

But I wasn't giving up that easily. "Oh yes, we will."

We started moving boxes and dragging bags aside as we moved deeper into the cellar. Suddenly Ewen almost jumped on top of me. "What was that noise?"

I could hear it too. A scratching, a squeaking, somewhere nearby. "I think it might be a mouse," I said, trying not to sound scared.

"Or . . . a rat?" Ewen suggested. He turned round, ready to head for the steps. "That's it, I'm out of here."

I grabbed him by the collar and dragged him back. "You're staying with me." Because I had seen what we were looking for: Granny Nothing's case.

There it was, lying on a shelf in the corner, gathering dust. We moved closer. There were labels from all sorts of exotic places. Mauritius, St Lucia, San Quentin, Troon.

"Troon. . . That sounds really exciting," Ewen said. "Wonder where it is?"

I pulled at the case frantically. "Let's get it opened."

There was the sound again. A scratching, louder and closer this time. We stood stock-still, listening. Expecting every moment to be rushed by a horde of hungry rats.

"It'll only be a tiny, tiny, microscopic mouse, probably." I was trying to convince myself as much as my brother.

"I don't care. I'm getting out of here."

I put the case on the ground and opened it with a flourish. It seemed to me that every time we looked inside that case we found something we had never seen before. But, of course, I knew that was impossible.

There was a voodoo mask that looked in the dim light as if the eyes were alive.

A boomerang with the words I'LL BE BACK etched into it.

A set of false teeth, grinning up at us.

A Sioux headdress made of feathers. Ewen moved it and immediately began to sneeze. Once he started, he couldn't stop.

"Shut up!" I said. "We're supposed to be quiet."

"I can't help it," he said, in between sneezes. "I'm allergic to feathers."

He was sneezing all over me, and all over the case. "Is that a big hankie?" he asked.

I told him it was and handed it to him. No point

telling him it was actually Granny Nothing's knickers. It would only make him sneeze even more.

"Right! Where is this key?" I pulled everything else aside, and there it was, looking even rustier than I remembered.

The Rusty Key.

She'd been terrified once when she thought we had taken it.

What was its secret?

Could it possibly open Mystico's Box of Mystery?

There was only one way to find out. I clutched it in my palm. "Come on, Ewen, time to go."

Ewen couldn't answer for sneezing. I stuffed everything back in the case, including Granny Nothing's knickers, now a bit wet.

And, still with that scratching in our ears, we sneaked back upstairs.

Chapter Ten

Next day, after school, Granny Nothing gathered us all together to take us to the carnival. And I mean all of us. Polly arrived with her sisters. They all looked like clones. Even Todd Dangerfield was there. The only two who were missing were Elvis and Presley. They were already at the carnival. "I'm fed up with going there!" Elvis kept saying. "But Nanny Sue drags us every day, just so she can be Mystico's assistant."

We weren't fed up with it, even if most of the acts

were rubbish. You could never be fed up when Granny Nothing was around.

Granny Nothing counted us all out. "Look at me," she said. "I'm like a lovely shepherdess with her little lambs." She called us all to attention. "Let's hit the road."

Dad looked lost. He stood holding two planks of wood and some nails. "What about me? Have I got to do this by myself?"

He sounded just like Ewen when he was feeling really sorry for himself.

"Don't be such a baby," Mum told him. "Just get on with it."

Granny Nothing was glorious today, a technicolour granny. Where did she get these dresses? This one looked just like the big top at the circus, a multicoloured tent with a bandana to match. Thomas, balanced on her head, was dressed exactly the same. Only at least he was wearing trousers.

I wished I had brought my sunglasses.

"Now, don't lose sight of Granny Nothing when we get to the carnival," she told everyone.

Ha! No fear of that. You could have spotted her from outer space.

The Great Alfredo certainly saw her. He started dancing about like a cat on an electrified tin roof.

"He's that happy to see me!" Granny Nothing actually sounded as if she believed that. "See, Steph, I have such a strange effect on men."

Alfredo pleaded with her. "Don't do anything. Please, don't do anything."

He was almost in tears. He came up to Granny Nothing's shoulders, which made him just the right height for Thomas to dribble all over him. I felt quite sorry for the poor soul.

"Och, don't get your jodphurs in a twist. I'm here for my children. I don't intend to do anything."

She shoved him aside, and he fell in a heap, knocking over the sign proclaiming:

COMING SOON. THE GREAT GORILLA. KING KONG HAS NOTHING ON HIM.

Granny Nothing had spotted the TEST YOUR STRENGTH stall. If you can ring the bell, you win a cuddly toy.

"Want it!" Thomas roared.

"You've got it, son," she said.

Personally I felt the man got entirely what he deserved. He should just have handed over the cuddly toy. Instead, he handed her the hammer. She swung it in the air, and brought it down. The ball raced up, rang the bell, and both the bell and the ball went into orbit. They're probably still circling the earth.

Granny Nothing handed Thomas his cuddly toy. The man hung up his "Out of Order" sign. The Great Alfredo screeched in horror.

"Granny, if you break anything else, we'll get barred."

"The Fun House!" Polly screamed.

And I thought, *Well, she couldn't actually break anything in there, could she?*

Oh yes, she could.

When she sat on the revolving chair, it collapsed and so did the revolving room.

In the haunted cellar we were attacked by an army of mechanical skeletons. A pathetic attempt to frighten us. Granny Nothing fought them all off and they ended up as a jangle of bones and wires all around the floor.

"We're just supposed to scream and run past them, Granny," I told her.

"Ooops," she said.

Polly came to a rolling path. "What's this?"

We soon found out. As we all weaved our way along it, it was hard to stand up straight. We were screaming and laughing as it rolled and rocked and sent us slipping and sliding. Halfway along the path a curtain suddenly opened and there we were, looking out on to the carnival where a whole crowd had gathered to watch the fun. At the same time, there was an upward draught which sent Polly's dress flying over her head. Polly screamed and yelled and tried to hold her dress down. The crowd loved it. They clapped and cheered. Granny Nothing stepped on to it before I could stop her. Her multicoloured big top fluttered and billowed over her head.

"I think I'm going to be sick," Ewen yelled. He wasn't the only one. People were covering their eyes, their mouths. Turning away as their faces went green. Some just looked on, stunned. However, the children loved it. Granny Nothing was wearing the biggest pair of bloomers I have ever seen. There were tents that size.

They had little white frills round the edges of the legs, to try to make them look a bit more feminine.

A losing battle.

She could have stuffed a small African country inside those knickers and still had room for a football team. And judging by her shape, she just might have done that already.

Granny Nothing thought it was brilliant. She was dancing about in delight. "Hell's Bells, I love the carnival!"

"Hell's Bells!" Thomas agreed, peering over the top of her dress.

I could see the Great Alfredo was in tears.

He fell down on the ground and put his head in his hands.

Frankly, I wasn't interested. It was if a spell had been woven round me again. All I wanted now was to go to the tent of Mystico the Mysterious.

I wanted to open the Box of Mystery.

Chapter Eleven

Mystico's tent was almost empty. Just a few bored-looking customers who'd come in out of the cold, and a little man picking his nose in a dark corner. There behind Mystico on the stage was the Box. One red spotlight was shining on it, catching the light from the diamonds and the rubies and the emeralds which encrusted it. I clutched the key even tighter in my hand.

Only one member of the audience looked enthralled. Nanny Sue. She stood gazing up at Mystico as if she was either hyptnotized, or madly in love. That was it.

She was in love with Mystico. I had visions of her running off with him. Sounded good to me.

"We must try and help this romance along, Ewen," I said. He was hardly listening. He was watching Mystico intently as he went through his routine of card tricks. "Think of a card, young man," he said to Ewen. His eyes bored into him. "And don't tell me what it is."

There was a drum roll, another puff of smoke . . . where did he get that smoke from? "Your card is . . . the nine of clubs!" He flung his arms wide, waiting for applause.

Ewen grinned from ear to ear. He beamed at me. He looked at Mystico. "No, it isn't," he said.

Mystico's jaw trembled. "Ah, I see. . ."

He covered his eyes with his cloak, he did a lot of moaning, then he threw the cloak from his face. "The ten of hearts!" he cried.

"Er . . . no," Ewen said again.

In the end Mystico went through 28 other cards before, getting really fed up, I said to my brother, "Oh, for goodness' sake, lie. Pretend. Or we'll all grow old and die in here."

"The Joker!" Ewen said in triumph to the crowd; all four of us. Everyone else had got bored and left. I didn't blame Mystico for being furious. I could have punched Ewen myself.

There was almost steam coming out of Mystico's ears.

"He's always this annoying, Mystico," cried Nanny Sue and she leapt on to the stage, her face beaming. "Would you like me to be your assistant again?"

By this time, Mystico looked completely fed up too. "Ah, it's you Stew," he said.

"It's Sue," she said, but he wasn't listening. For something else had caught his attention. I was holding up the Rusty Key.

"I want to try to open the Box," I said.

Mystico's eyes flashed. "Ah, you think you can open my Box of Mystery," he said, peering at the key. He looked disappointed. It did look a bit tatty, and even rustier than I remembered. And it had bits of the Sioux headdress stuck to it too. "With that?"

"It's a key, isn't it?"

He hesitated. "It's a rusty key," he said.

"I want to try," I insisted.

"Don't let her, Mystico," Nanny Sue tugged at his cloak and half a pack of cards fell out. "Saw me in half instead."

Now that was tempting, but as I pointed out to Mystico, he could still do that after we'd opened the Box.

He turned to Nanny Sue. "Bring forth the Box!" he commanded.

Nanny Sue had a lot of trouble bringing it forth. She pushed, she pulled, she dragged it. It looked heavy. I had visions of it filled with real diamonds and gold and rubies and emeralds. First thing I would do is have a tiara made, maybe two. One for school. Finally, she set it down in front of Mystico, and collapsed on the stage, breathless.

"Now, bring forth the key!" Mystico said in a deep

voice. At the same time he snapped his fingers and a puff of green smoke filled the stage. Nanny Sue immediately started coughing.

I clambered on to the stage. So did Ewen. Before I passed him the key, however, I asked Mystico, "We definitely get to keep whatever is in the Box?"

"Whatever is in the Box!" he said greedily.

"And we keep the money?" Ewen asked.

Mystico flashed the notes in front of us. "You keep the money."

"So . . . what do you get out of this?" I asked him.

It was as if his eyes became great moons of mystery. "Everything my heart desires," he said.

"They'll never open anything with that rusty key, Mystico," Nanny Sue warned him. "You're losing your audience." And he was – only the little man with a finger halfway up his nose was left watching us intently. "Saw me in half," Nanny Sue insisted.

"Later," Mystico promised.

I bent down and slipped the key in the lock. This was it. Would the key open the Box? And what could possibly be inside?

Outside the tent I could hear the sounds of the carnival, music from the rides, screams from people on the dodgems, the smells of toffee apples and greasy hamburgers.

I took a deep breath and turned the key.

And the Box opened.

Chapter Twelve

Ewen stared into the empty Box. "There's nothing in it," he said. He felt all around the inside. "There's nothing there."

But there had to be. My vision of sitting in class wearing a tiara of rubies and diamonds and precious jewels was fading by the second.

"Maybe there's a secret compartment," I said. I didn't add that a secret compartment was exactly where a treasure map would be hidden. I didn't want to sound stupid. Luckily, that's never held my brother back.

"There might be a treasure map," he said.

We thumped the Box, we bashed the Box. We even got inside the Box and jumped all over it. Nothing made any difference. It was just a Box.

"It's empty," I said.

"I never said anything different," Mystico answered. And that's when I noticed something strange. Mystico was grinning as if something wonderful had happened.

"Why are you looking so happy?" I asked him. "There's nothing in the Box."

He really did have scary eyes. He flashed them at me. "Nothing you can see," he said mysteriously. Then he began to laugh. He laughed so much I was sure he was going to wet himself. He was in hysterics. He laughed so much he began to frighten me. Even the strange little man in the corner stopped picking his nose to watch him.

"He's dotty," Ewen said, and it's not often I agree with my brother.

"Let's get out of here."

Ewen held out his hand for the money he had been promised. He certainly wasn't leaving without that.

"Before you go," Mystico said. "One more trick."

I'd had enough of his rubbish tricks but before we could take a step off the stage, Mystico stuck his hand into his hat.

"Here we go, another blinking bunny rabbit."

But when he drew his hand from the hat it wasn't a bunny rabbit at all. It was a puppy, and then, he pulled out a kitten, and then, how we gasped! he pulled out a baby crocodile.

In fact, that seemed to take Mystico by surprise too.

"How did he do that?" Ewen asked. "He's usually rubbish."

Nanny Sue put her arms around his neck. "Mystico, you are magnificent." She gazed up at him with adoring eyes. "I will stay with you for ever."

But Mystico wasn't listening. He held the tiny struggling crocodile high in the air and he began to laugh again.

"It has begun!" he cried. "The world is mine!"

"He really is crazy," I said to Ewen, and I pulled him out of the tent.

Outside, the weather had gone wild. The wind had suddenly become a hurricane and it whipped leaves and chairs and cartons and rubbish all across the ground. One of the banners heralding the carnival had snapped and it billowed across the sky. From somewhere nearby we could hear screams and yells and shouts of panic.

"What's happening?" Ewen cried as we ran towards the shouting. We turned a corner and there was everyone, jumping scratching, screeching. . .

The Great Alfredo had fainted. Baldy was jumping about too. But he looked happy. "I have made a stand for the dumb animals of the world!" he was yelling. "I have freed the first animals."

"You idiot!" A woman, jumping about madly too, thumped him with her handbag. "You didn't have to start with the flea circus."

Now I knew why everyone was jumping about.

Suddenly, so was I. Something nipped my leg, then my neck, then my belly. I began to scratch and scream.

"You and your bee in your bonnet about animal rights!" The woman walloped Baldy again and sent him reeling across the ground.

Well, now along with a bee in his bonnet, he had a flea up his trousers. A few thousand of them.

The only ones who weren't jumping about were Granny Nothing and Thomas. Probably even the fleas knew that if they landed on her it would be a suicide mission. In fact, quite a few fleas had obviously tried it and were lying round her feet, unconscious. Thomas was safe too, perched on her shoulders and screaming with delight as he watched the fun.

"Hell's Bells!" he was yelling.

Granny Nothing was having a great time. "This takes me back to my days in the Mexican jumping-bean factory!"

The Great Alfredo opened his eyes. He sat up and looked around him. He'd obviously been hoping it had all been a dream. His face went deathly pale.

"Why did I ever come to this town? You are killing my carnival!" His eyes went wide as a swarm of fleas headed towards him.

"AAAAAAGGHHH!" he screamed. And then he fainted again.

Chapter Thirteen

All the way home, the wind howled through the trees, dragging golden leaves from branches and sending them spinning through the air like tops. Polly kept being lifted off her feet and only Granny Nothing grabbing her kept her from spinning off too. The wind whipped at Elvis's coat and a couple of times he looked as if he was about to take off. Presley gripped on to his trousers with his teeth and held him down.

Nanny Sue was being bashed about all over the place. One minute she was banging her head off a wall, the next she was thrown across the pavement and almost knocked herself out on a lamp post. "Agh! This is worse than the big wheel!" she screamed.

"That wind only started when the Box was opened," Ewen whispered.

"Rubbish!" I told him. "It's only wind." My brother is always looking for a mystery. "The Box was empty . . . like your head."

When we got back home, Mum was in a panic. "Thank goodness you're here! Your dad dug a hole in the conservatory and fell right through to the cellar. He's still dangling there. I've been trying to get him out for an hour."

Goodness! We only leave him for an afternoon and he ends up dangling in the cellar. Now I know where Ewen gets it from.

"I'll get him," Granny Nothing said, pushing up her sleeves and lumbering towards the conservatory. "He's useless." She said it almost with a touch of pride, I thought. "He gets that from his faither's side of the family."

Now, there was something I had never considered. That my dad had a "faither". That meant that someone must have fancied Granny Nothing enough to marry her. What kind of man would be brave enough to do that? One without a brain obviously.

Dad was hanging by one hand from the conservatory floor, his feet dangling into the cellar. "Thank goodness," he said breathlessly. "I can't hold on for much longer."

Granny Nothing swung him up to safety with one yank. He fell on the ground, exhausted. "I was scared down there. I kept hearing funny noises."

And I remembered the funny noises Ewen and I had heard when we had taken the Rusty Key from Granny Nothing's case.

Granny Nothing brushed him down tenderly. "You leave the heavy stuff to me, son," she said. "I don't want you hurting yourself."

Mum tutted loudly. "Can't even dig a hole without falling through it!" She stomped into the living room.

I had to agree with her. "Honestly, Dad, you are useless."

Ewen stood beside him loyally. But then, he's useless too.

That night I woke up with the strangest feeling of unease. I took out my earplugs. We all wore them, specially reinforced – Dad had bought us a job lot – to block out Granny Nothing's snoring.

Something had woken me. The wind was still howling outside, though it was drowned out by Granny Nothing's snores. But there was another sound, coming from downstairs. A sound I hadn't heard before. A rustling noise, as if all the autumn leaves had blown into our living room. Had Dad left a door open before we went to bed? That would be just like him.

I got out of bed, and began to creep downstairs.

Was I afraid it might be burglars? Now, why should I be afraid of burglars with Granny Nothing in the house? We'd had burglars before and she'd convinced them to make a career change. They were lollipop men these days.

I stood at the bottom of the stairs and listened to the sounds coming from the living room. I imagined thousands of crackly golden leaves being whisked all over our good furniture. I turned the handle of the door, and pushed it open.

The room was dark.

And the floor was moving.

But not with autumn leaves.

Scores of tiny eyes turned on me. For a moment, a split second, the rustling, squeaking sound stopped.

I broke the silence. I screamed so loud I broke a window.

Our living room was full of mice.

They were on the floor. They were scratching about on the table. They were scuttling all over the sofa and the armchairs. They were everywhere.

I didn't stop screaming.

Dad was the first one downstairs. He took one look into the living room and yelled. Next thing I knew, he was standing on a chair. "There's hundreds of them!"

Mum was next. And she leapt on the chair with him before you could say, "MICE!"

As soon as Ewen saw the writhing mass in the living room he was on top of them both, hanging on to Dad's neck like a sailor clinging to the mast of a sinking ship.

Then Granny Nothing came down. "Right! I'll sort this out. Lucky for yous I was the rat catcher in Rio de

January." She swung Thomas from her shoulders and handed him to Mum. "Here. Hold my boy!" Then she pushed up her sleeves and charged into the living room like a rampaging elephant, hauling the door shut behind her.

We could hear squealing, and screeching and yelling and stamping and stomping and squelching.

"Oh my goodness. There's too many of them. They'll over run her. They'll eat her alive!" Mum screamed.

She'd be more likely to poison them, I thought. I wasn't worried. Whatever was happening in there I knew that Granny Nothing would be getting the better of those mice.

Ten minutes later she flung the door open. She was covered in sweat and had a couple of dead mice attached to her hair. "They've gone," she said triumphantly.

Our celebrations were shortlived. From somewhere in the street there was a sudden scream of horror. It sounded like Mrs Scoular. We all ran outside just as she was scuttling out of her house in her nightdress, followed by hundreds of mice.

Granny Nothing was there in a flash. She can move fast for a woman as big as a tank. She swung Mrs Scoular over her shoulder and carried her back into our house and deposited her in Dad's arms.

"I only went downstairs for a drink of water . . . and they were all there, waiting for me," Mrs Scoular wailed.

Granny Nothing was after them again. This time they made for the Singhs' house. Minutes later Nanny Sue appeared, running wildly on her spindly splayed legs. Mice were clinging to the hem of her nightie like tassles. The Singhs were running too, but they were laughing as if it was great fun. I noticed too that they'd brought their guitars. I groaned at the thought of another singing session.

Then Granny Nothing reappeared from their house. She had Elvis under one arm and Presley under the other. She pelted into our hallway.

"Right! I've got them cornered. Leave this to me."

Then she was gone, lumbering and roaring back to the Singhs'.

"She's an inspiration!" Mrs Singh said. Then she turned to her husband. "My dear, we must write a song about Granny Nothing."

And they did. Then and there.

And then they sang it. Over . . . and over . . . and over.

You know, I think I would have preferred being eaten by the mice.

Buzz

Buzz

Chapter Fourteen

"It's all your fault!" Mum turned on Dad. "You and your conservatory! You dug that hole too deep and out they came."

"How was I to know they were there?" Dad said meekly.

"Lucky Granny Nothing was here. Or we would have been eaten alive by mice."

"I think mice are vegetarian, dear," Dad said, but Mum wasn't listening. She was too busy surveying the mess her living room was in.

Nanny Sue was wailing in a corner. Everyone ignored her. "I've had a terrible shock! I think I might need counselling to recover." I noticed a stray mouse sneak up her nightie. I decided not to tell her. The mouse would get a bigger shock than she would.

Mrs Scoular was shaking and rattling like a skeleton. "It's all Granny Nothing's fault. Strange things have been happening ever since she came here."

That wasn't the way Granny Nothing saw it. She stomped back to the house, dusted herself down and beamed at us. "Sorted!" she said.

By next day, we had another problem.

Mum was in the kitchen putting the last touches to our Hallowe'en costumes. Dad was hammering loudly in his "conservative", and Granny Nothing was on all fours searching for Thomas under the autumn leaves that carpetted our garden.

"Come to your granny, darlin'," she was calling.

And I could hear Thomas somewhere roaring with laughter.

With any luck she'd never find him.

Ewen and I were upstairs, doing our homework. We both heard it at the same time.

A buzzing.

"What is that?" Ewen asked.

Then we saw it, a solitary wasp buzzing around lazily at the open window.

"It must be lonely," Ewen said, full of sympathy. "All the wasps are finished for the summer. It must be the last of its kind, poor thing."

At that moment there was another buzzing. The last of its kind had a friend. And then another. And then another. And another.

I looked at Ewen. He looked at me.

"Where are they all coming from?"

It didn't matter where they were coming from. I was sure I knew exactly where they were headed. Me! I jumped out of my seat and my homework scattered everywhere. I screamed. The room was suddenly alive with wasps, buzzing, hovering, diving.

"Granny Nothing!" I screamed.

She was there in an instant. Mum and Dad behind her.

"There must be a wasp's nest outside the window," Dad said. "I'll phone the pest people." And he was gone.

"No time for that!" Granny Nothing said. "Leave it to me."

The wasps must have seen her mountain of flesh and thought it was a gift from wasp heaven, just for them.

They divebombed at her, but it was a kamikaze mission. As soon as they hit her, they were out for the count. One by one. They landed on Granny Nothing and it was all over for them.

At least it was quick.

It occurred to me that if we could bottle whatever it was she had and sell it, we could make our fortune.

By the time Dad came back it was all over. "They're on their way," he said, beaming a smile. Then he noticed the carpet of dead wasps at Granny Nothing's enormous feet. "Oh," he said, weakly.

Mum sniffed. "As usual, Granny Nothing handled it."

But it wasn't his fault this time . . . or was it? Was it all his hammering which had awakened the wasps in their nest?

Granny Nothing crunched towards us. "Get me a couple of shovels. We'll give these poor things a decent burial."

"Didn't they sting you?" Ewen asked, amazed.

"Me? No, son. You see when I was working in the Australian bushes, I met up with the Granny Nothing of Queen Wasps. It was a battle to the death. She stung me that many times that my blood is immune to any wasp sting. In fact, it'll kill them dead at twenty paces."

Another of her stories! "I think it's just called the Bush," I corrected her.

She shook her head. "Oh no, Steph. It's a big country. I think there must be more than one."

That night, Ewen crept into my room. "First the mice, and then the wasps. Come on, Steph. You've got to agree. Strange things have been happening since we opened that Box."

"Get real, Ewen. Dad dug a hole, and disturbed the mice. He was making too much noise and he annoyed the wasps. It is all perfectly logical."

He was having none of that. "No. It's since that Box was opened. It's not Dad's fault. It's ours."

"Watch my lips, Ewen. The Box was empty."

But of course, he wouldn't listen. He wanted a mystery.

The only mystery was how he managed to be so thick!

However, over the next couple of days, I began to wonder if he was right. . .

Chapter Fifteen

We all went to the carnival again the next day. The gorilla had arrived at last and everyone wanted to see it. Would it be as fierce as the Great Alfredo had promised? However, the real reason why Ewen and I wanted to go was to see if anything had changed for Mystico.

It certainly had. Mystico's tent was filled to capacity – about the only thing at the carnival that was drawing the crowds. The rest of the carnival looked pretty pathetic. The fat lady was losing weight with the worry of it all, and the bearded lady could still only manage some designer stubble.

But people were crowding into Mystico's tent, before moving on to see this famous gorilla.

"He looks different," I said to Ewen. And he did. There was an evil glint in those eyes now. And his teeth looked like fangs.

The most amazing thing was that, for the first time, his tricks worked.

He guessed everyone's card without a moment's hesitation. He pulled all sorts of strange and wonderful things from his top hat, and from beneath his cloak. He was impressing everyone.

Nanny Sue was there too, gazing up at him with adoring eyes. As soon as he called out for a beautiful assistant she leapt up on to the stage, battling it out with two other girls for the privilege. She threw off her overcoat and underneath she was dressed in a pink tutu and tights. The tights were all wrinkly on her skinny legs and the tutu didn't fit either. She looked like a worn-out fairy from the top of the Christmas tree. "I'll be your beautiful assistant," she simpered.

Mystico didn't look entirely delighted about that. "Ah, it's the lovely Stew again. . ."

Nanny Sue tried to correct him. "I'm the lovely Sue," but once again, he ignored her.

"Saw her in half!" This time it was Elvis who suggested it. Presley let out a howl of agreement.

Mystico obviously hadn't mastered the sawing-in-half

thing, because he only made her disappear again. This time it worked to perfection. He drew back the cubicle curtain and Nanny Sue had gone. I expected her to make an unsightly entrance, perhaps through the roof this time. But no. Mystico closed the curtain, said the magic words, "the Magic of Mystico," and a moment later there was Nanny Sue standing inside the cubicle looking slightly dazed. "Where have I been?" she asked.

"Look, there's the Box," Ewen whispered as Mystico took his bow.

There it lay, still open, right at the back of the stage.

"He's only had these magic powers since we opened that Box." Ewen was sure of it.

"He hasn't got any magic powers, stupid. He does tricks."

"But he gets them right now." And I couldn't argue with him there.

Everyone was impressed with Mystico as we left the tent. "He's certainly been practising," they were all saying. And: "He's about the only good thing at this carnival."

But, of course, we still had to see this famous gorilla.

The sign outside the tent proclaimed his arrival: GORDON THE GORILLA. COME AND SEE HIM. IF YOU DARE.

Gordon! I mean they might have given him a scarier name than Gordon. First, Sydney the boa constrictor and now, Gordon the gorilla! I ask you.

"Do you think it will be as big as King Kong?" Ewen asked me.

"He would hardly be likely to fit in a tent then, would he?"

Granny Nothing had taken Thomas to the kiddie car ride. "My wee boy would be scared of a big gorilla. I'm not having that."

Ha! He spent his days with Granny Nothing. A mountain of gorillas wouldn't scare him after that.

The crowd who bulged into the tent were noisy and excited. Right at the front, on the stage, was a cage. It seemed to stretch deep into the darkness at the back of the tent.

"Where's the gorilla?" Ewen asked, peering closer.

Suddenly all the lights went out and there was a gasp from the crowd.

"Can you see anything?" Ewen was practically clambering on to my shoulders, Elvis was climbing on his, and even Presley was getting in on the act.

All at once there was a roar from deep in the cage and the gorilla appeared from the blackness and charged towards the front. Everyone screamed and stepped back as it grabbed the bars and rattled them ferociously.

"Do you think that cage is safe?" Ewen asked.

I was glad that we were so far at the back now, but I couldn't let him see I was worried. "Of course it is. Do you think it's going to suddenly break free?"

Boys are so stupid.

Gordon the gorilla lumbered back into the shadows as if he was fed up with us. Everyone peered closer to see what he was doing.

There was another great roar and once again he charged to the front of the cage. He grabbed at the bars. He rattled them furiously. No one stepped back this time.

Bad move.

For this time, the bars didn't hold. The cage door burst open, and with another wild roar, Gordon the gorilla was free!

Grrr

Chapter Sixteen

The place went mental. Everyone screamed in panic and rushed for the exit. I grabbed Ewen and Elvis and hauled them along with me to safety. Presley was out before any of us.

Granny Nothing was waiting outside the tent. It was hard not to notice that she had a kiddie car wrapped round her middle. "They make these things far too wee," she was telling anyone who would listen as they panicked past her. She'd obviously just demolished another of the Great Alfredo's rides. However, she was alert in an instant when she saw us running out of the tent. Her eyes went wide. "What's going on here!"

Ewen leapt on to her. "Granny, it's the gorilla. He's escaped."

She straightened up, towering above us. She was like Godzilla. "Right!" she said. "Hold my boy!" And with that she shoved Thomas into my arms. She pushed up her sleeves, always a sign she means business. "Where is he?"

Everyone pointed at the tent. "In there!"

Everyone expected Granny Nothing to save the day. It was at that very moment, Gordon the gorilla (Honestly! Gordon!) emerged from his tent. He was still roaring and pounding his chest with his fists. Then he lumbered towards us with his arms swinging on the ground.

Granny Nothing tutted. "Mind you, he should never have been in a cage in the first place," she said. However, he had been frightening her children, and for anything man or beast, that was something she never tolerated.

She charged at Gordon. She roared at him, and Gordon could never compete with that roar. She lifted him with one hand and shook him. Then she grabbed him by the throat and began to throttle him.

"She's really good at throttling, isn't she?" Elvis said, his voice full of admiration.

"That's my granny," Ewen said with pride.

Now she was swinging Gordon around her head like a carousel. His roar had become a whimper. A cry that sounded almost human. I began to feel sorry for him.

Nanny Sue was writing furiously in her notebook – "cruelty to animals", probably.

Then the most terrifying thing happened. The crowd let out an unearthly scream as Gordon's head flew off ! It spun through the air, and smacked Nanny Sue right in the kisser. She began to dance around in a panic.

Ewen gingerly lifted the head from the ground. He squeaked. I could hardly look, expecting blood to be dripping from the neck, brains dribbling out, maybe a couple of eyeballs. Well, you would, wouldn't you?

Instead, it was flat. Ewen peeked inside. "There's nothing there," he said. "It's empty."

We all looked back at Gordon the gorilla. But now, to our astonishment, it was the Great Alfredo's head which was peeking out of a gorilla body.

"Let me down, please," his tinny little voice squeaked.

Even Granny Nothing was puzzled. She lowered him to the ground. "What's going on here?" she demanded.

The gorilla with the Great Alfredo's head crumpled to the ground. His face was green. No, grey. No, chalk white. Then it was green again.

The Great Alfredo began to cry. "Gordon the gorilla was going to save my carnival. He was going to be a great attraction. The only one who is doing any business is Mystico. And now he wants to buy me out. But I won't sell. Gordon was going to save me."

"So, where is Gordon?" I asked.

"He was unavoidably detained," Alfredo said pitifully.

"So I thought, I'll pretend to be him. No one will know the difference."

I noticed that Nanny Sue was scribbling frantically – "cruelty to humans" now, probably. That is, if you could call Alfredo human.

"Mystico wants to buy the carnival," I heard her mutter. "A wedding present for me, no doubt."

Ewen held out the gorilla mask to Alfredo. "Here's your head back," he said.

Alfredo turned his big sad eyes on Granny Nothing. He noticed – who could miss it? – that she was still attached to a kiddie car. "That's another ride you've broken, I suppose."

She lifted him to his feet. "Och, Alfredo, you've got to look on the bright side. Things could get a lot worse."

She was so right. They could . . . and they did.

Chapter Seventeen

Next day brought yet another problem. Ewen woke up, moaning and clutching at his stomach. He got out of bed and ran for the toilet. He couldn't get in. Mum was already there. Her moans were louder than his. I was rubbing at my eyes as I came out of the bedroom to find a queue. Dad was jumping up and down. Ewen was pounding on the bathroom door.

"What's the matter?" I asked sleepily.

"Dia . . . dia . . . dia. . ." Ewen stumbled over the word. "I've got the runs."

"I've got the runs," Dad repeated.

Mum moaned from inside the bathroom.

"How do you feel, Steph?" Dad asked me.

"I feel as fit as a fiddle!" (What a daft thing to say. How fit is a fiddle?)

Granny Nothing emerged from her room with Thomas wrapped round her neck like a scarf. She was wearing an all-in-one sleepsuit. All red and yellow twirls and stripes.

Dad took one look and his face turned green. "I'm going to faint just looking at that." He shut his eyes.

"Not here, Dad," Ewen said. "There's no room. You'll fall on top of me."

"I feel fine," I said again.

"Stephanie's just like her granny. Constitution like an ox."

Why does she always say these things! I am not like her at all.

"They've got a bug," I told her.

"It would be all that junk they ate at the carnival," she said wisely. "Toffee apples and candyfloss and greasy hamburgers and hot dogs with mustard and tomato sauce all over them."

Dad turned an even stranger shade of green. "Stop!" he yelled. "Don't say another word. I feel sick."

"So do I." Ewen's face was as white as a sheet in a detergent advert. Together they looked like a Celtic flag.

"Leave this to me," Granny Nothing said. "I've got the perfect cure."

Dad seemed to turn even greener. "What do you mean?"

Granny Nothing gently placed Thomas in my arms, giving him a big wet kiss on the cheek. Thomas gurgled happily. "Hold my boy," she said. "I am going to make up my magic medicine."

Ewen began to tremble. "Your magic . . . what?"

Dad looked terrified. "Oh, no," he pleaded.

"Oh aye, son, and with Granny Nothing's special ingredient."

Dad tried to stand up straight. "No. Honestly. I feel better already."

"See what I mean by magic!" Granny Nothing squeezed his cheeks. "Just the thought of my special ingredient always made you feel better." And she waddled off happily.

Dad waited until she was gone. "She's right. I was always too terrified of getting it ever to admit to feeling ill."

"Is it that bad?" Ewen asked him.

Dad put his hand on Ewen's shoulder. "You're going to have to be brave, son."

Whatever the special ingredient was, it was, as always, green.

Dad backed away from her as she came towards him holding a spoon dripping with the green glowing liquid.

Yes. It actually glowed.

Now, that can't be good for you.

"Open your mouth, son."

Dad refused. He pursed his lips and shook his head and backed into a corner.

Granny Nothing grabbed him by the nose and squeezed hard. He had no choice. It was either die, or open his mouth. As soon as he did, the green goo was pushed in.

"There ye are," she said. "You'll be as right as rain tomorrow."

Right as rain! Another stupid staying. What does that mean?

Ewen was harder to handle. He squirmed and he struggled but she clamped him under one arm and forced the spoon between his lips.

"This is cruelty to children!" he yelled.

"It's called tough love!" Granny Nothing yelled back

Mum locked herself in the bathroom, but that didn't stop Granny Nothing. She picked the lock.

"My spell working undercover with that gang of safe crackers wasn't wasted," she said, dragging Mum across the bathroom tiles and forcing the spoon into her mouth. Dad was right about one thing. There was no way I intended to be ill now.

It turned out that the whole street was affected. Granny Nothing was delighted. "I can cure them all," she said. "I'm like a doctor in the jungle saving everybody's lives."

"That would be a witch-doctor."

But she wasn't listening. She was on a mission.

She started with the Singhs. They refused point blank to open their mouths. So she asked them to entertain her with an Elvis song. She had the spoon in their mouths before you could say "Jailhouse Rock".

Elvis and Presley went into hiding, but she knew they couldn't stay put for long. She grabbed both of them as they sneaked to the toilet.

Nanny Sue was the best fun. Granny Nothing gave her three spoonfuls . . . just to show there were no hard feelings.

That night Granny Nothing was feeling pretty pleased with herself. "You know, Steph, I was definitely put in this wurruld to solve people's problems."

She actually believed that.

That same night Ewen crept into my room. "You must know what caused all this illness," he said.

"Candyfloss," I told him. "Or fizzy lemonade. Or hamburgers dripping with grease?"

Ewen was beginning to look sick again. He shook his head.

I knew what he was going to say. "The Box. Since we opened that Box there has been one disaster after another."

"Rubbish!" I said. The Box had been empty. That had disappointed me, but I refused to believe opening that Box had changed anything.

"You wait and see," he said. "Something else is going to happen, and then you'll have to believe me."

Chapter Eighteen

The wind whipped the leaves from the trees and whistled through the branches. Clouds scuttled across an eggshell moon. It was a perfect Hallowe'en night.

Thanks to Granny Nothing's green medicine, everyone was fit and healthy again. At least, she was taking all the credit for it. She collected all the children from their homes before we started doing our trick-or-treating. Granny Nothing was our bodyguard. We were safer than houses.

Polly was dressed as an executioner, complete with plastic axe and a severed head dripping with blood. Honestly, for such a sweet-looking little girl she has a very strange imagination. Todd Dangerfield was coming with us too. Todd, once arch enemy number one, seemed to always want to be in our company these days. "I'm turning over a new leaf," he kept telling us. He was dressed as a baby. He was wearing a nappy and had a dummy in his mouth. Hopefully, it would keep him quiet all night.

Elvis looked really grand in a red silk kaftan and was wearing a turban like a maharajah.

"You're a maharajah?" I asked. He was quite offended.

"I'm a Bollywood film star!" he said. Presley was like the Bollywood version of Greyfriars Bobby, following Elvis and wearing a matching turban tied on to his sparkly collar.

"We've got to get used to dressing like this. We're going to be big stars."

Presley grinned up at him. Can dogs grin? Presley certainly could. Bonkers, both of them.

We waited for Ewen to make his entrance. He was the Incredible Hulk. Bulging muscles and green skin which looked very authentic. I began to wonder if it had anything to do with Granny Nothing's medicine.

And me? I was a beautiful fairy. All dressed in pink. Light on my tiny, neat and petite feet, with stars in my hair and carrying a wand.

Polly ran up to me. "You look brilliant, Steph," she

said. And I beamed at her. "You look just like Granny Nothing."

I was shocked, horrified, mortified, petrified. I jumped up and down. "I'm a fairy! I'm a fairy!" I screamed.

Todd Dangerfield took the dummy out of his mouth. "Of course you are. You're Granny Nothing dressed up as a fairy." He grinned at everyone. "Definite family resemblance, eh?"

That was it. I charged at him and we both fell to the ground. I started battering him with my wand and he was hitting me with his rattle. It was a fight to the death.

Granny Nothing separated us and lifted us both in the air. Me by my wings, and she lifted Todd by his nappy and gave him a wedgie.

"Och, Stephanie, my darling. We're just going to have to accept it. You can't disguise beauty. And we're more gorgeouser than anybody else."

She would never learn English! "We're more gorgeous! Gorgeous! Gorgeous!" I corrected.

"That's what I just said," she agreed. Then she opened her mouth so wide to laugh I could see her breakfast. Egg on toast, I think.

Granny Nothing set out her plan for the evening. "We'll go round the houses, and then we'll all come back here for one of my finger buffets."

She pronounced "buffet" to rhyme with "muffet" as in Little Miss. There was no point correcting her, and heaven knows whose fingers she planned to use for her "finger" buffet.

We made a crocodile round the houses and, thanks to Granny Nothing, we made a lot of money too. At first Mrs Scoular refused to let us in, but Granny Nothing threatened to huff and to puff and to blow her house down. The old skinflint didn't even have any nuts or apples or anything for us. All she gave us was a gingernut, and I think that had been in her cupboard for years.

One of our new neighbours at the end of the street opened her door, took one look at Granny Nothing and fainted with fright. Her husband came running to revive her. "No wonder she fainted," he said to Granny Nothing. "That mask is far too scary."

Granny Nothing threw her head back and laughed. "God luv ye, this is no' a mask. This is my real face." Then he fainted too.

As we walked along the street, Nanny Sue appeared and grabbed Elvis. "Come on, we're going to the carnival."

Elvis pulled away from her. "I'm fed up with going to the carnival. The only thing I want to go on is the big dipper and it's broken."

I snapped at her. "Leave him be! He doesn't want to go."

She snapped back. "Shut up you! If he doesn't go, I don't get to go either." Her eyes went all misty. "This could be my last chance of happiness. I think Mystico's going to ask me to run away with him."

My eyes lit up. Ewen's eyes lit up. Elvis's eyes lit up. Presley began panting happily. I put my hand on Elvis's shoulder. "Go. It's in a good cause." And it was. We might just get rid of Nanny Sue for good.

We were on our way home to sample Granny Nothing's "finger buffet" when suddenly the whole street was plunged into darkness.

"It's a power cut," Polly said, and she clung to Granny Nothing's wrinkled legs.

"Everything seems to be happening around here at the moment," Todd Dangerfield said. "First the mice, then the wasps, then everybody getting sick. You would think somebody had put a spell on the place."

"It's the Box again, Steph," Ewen whispered.

By the light of the moon I could see Granny Nothing's face. She looked troubled. "Something's wrong here," she said. "My corns are going crazy and when my corns go crazy it can only mean one thing." She paused dramatically, then she roared. "The wurruld is out of whack!"

oops

Chapter Nineteen

The wind howled around her, and the moon, as if on cue, suddenly appeared from behind the clouds and cast an eerie silver glow on Granny Nothing's warts. It was as if they became alive.

"The wurruld," she repeated, "is out of whack!"

"The *world* is out of whack," I corrected her.

She stared at me. "Aye, you feel it the same as me, Steph. Are your corns acting up a well?"

I was affronted. "I haven't got corns!"

She nodded wisely. "You will. You're just like Granny."

I promised myself I would never have great big corns like hers. I would have neat and petite feet. I would go to a chiropodist everyday to make sure of it. Starting tomorrow.

"It's our fault, Stephanie." Ewen pulled at my sleeve.

Granny Nothing bent down. "What was that, son?"

"He's talking rubbish," I said.

"No, I am not!"

"Tell your granny, son."

Thomas roared in agreement. "Tell your grrranny." Though he hadn't a clue what he was saying.

"We opened the Box, Granny. Me and Stephanie. We took the Rusty Key and we opened Mystico's Box of Mystery."

He babbled out the whole story. Ewen would never make a secret agent. He couldn't keep his mouth shut for a minute.

Granny Nothing started swaying. She clasped her hands together and began to pray. "Oh, no, anything but that. Not the Rusty Key. Not that. There's only one Box that key can open. Tell me you never opened that Box. Naw. Naw. Naw."

Thomas, attached to her neck, swayed along with her. "Naw, naw, naw." He dribbled all through her hair.

Ewen was almost in tears. "It's all our fault, Granny. Me and Steph's."

"No, darlin'. Don't blame yourself. That Mystico's put you under his evil spell. I know the type."

"What is the secret of the Rusty Key, Granny?" Ewen asked, seriously.

We all stood around her in the moonlight as she began to tell her story – another of them. Polly sat on her severed head, and Todd Dangerfield sucked frantically on his dummy.

"It's a strange and wonderful story," she began.

"Aren't they all?" I muttered, but nobody listened.

"Shut up, Steph." Ewen glowed a threatening shade of green in the moonlight. So I shut up. Anyway, to be honest, I wanted to hear the story too.

"It all began in Martinique." (She pronounced it Martineekie.) "That's in the Caribbean. A strange and wonderful island, full of colour and voodoo and magic . . . and a nice wee line in silk scarves."

Ewen screeched so loud I thought Sydney had come back and tried to eat him. "Martinique! Granny, that's where Mystico said he got the Box."

Granny Nothing was nodding so hard that her teeth, all four of them, were rattling in her mouth. "I thought as much. My corns are never wrong."

"So, what happened in Martinique?" I asked, as eager now to find out as everyone else.

"Strange and weird things had been happening when I got there, just like here. The island was overrun by snakes, there was a plague of scorpions and lager louts. The tourist trade was taking an awful bashing. The wurruld was out of whack. The people were a-wailing and a-praying for a saviour to come along and save them . . . and that very day I arrived on the half-past-four ferry."

"Granny Nothing, what would the world do without you?" Polly said.

Granny Nothing beamed, and the moonlight caught on one of her remaining teeth and it seemed to flash like something out of a cartoon. "I know," she said, "I sometimes wonder that myself."

Modesty is not one of Granny Nothing's virtues.

"Well, the voodoo chief came to me," she went on. "He had tried everything, he said, and then he told me about the Box."

"The Box?" Ewen asked.

"Have you heard of Pandora?" Granny Nothing asked.

Todd Dangerfield pulled out his dummy. "I know her. She lives round the corner from me."

I walloped him with my wand again. "Not that Pandora, stupid!" I looked at Granny Nothing. "You mean Pandora, who was given a Box and told never to look inside?"

I had read of the old legend in my Girls' Book of Strange Stories.

Granny Nothing nodded. "Aye, and typical female, she was too nosey for her own good. She opened the Box and every evil known to mankind was released. War, famine, drought, and bad feet. "She almost wept at the thought of it. "That's what had happened on Martineekie. The Box had been opened. The wurruld had to be saved. I had to get that key and lock the Box again. You know, it was one of the hardest jobs I've ever had."

"So where did you find the key?" Polly asked.

"Well, it's rusty, so it must have been in water somewhere," I suggested.

Ewen was sitting with his mouth hanging open. He

looked like a fish. "I know! You had to dive for it, into the blue waters of the Caribbean. It was guarded by a giant octopus. You fought it off." At this stage, he was dancing around, slicing off imaginary tentacles with an imaginary sword. "You fought it off, cutting off each tentacle one by one, until it ran away in terror."

"It would hardly run with no tentacles left, stupid," I said. "It would be more likely to roll."

He wasn't interested in logic. "Is that where you found the key, Granny?" he asked her. "In the deep clear waters of the Caribbean?"

"Not at all," she said. "It was stuck down the toilet pan in a local bar. Lucky it hadn't been flushed away or we'd never have got it."

I began to feel sick. I had handled something that had been down a toilet pan!

"Then, it was a race against time to get that Box shut again."

"Why was that, Granny?"

"Because that Box had to be shut before midnight on the thirty-first of October, or it would stay open for ever and the evil would stay in the wurruld."

Polly tugged at Granny Nothing's sleeve.

"What is it, pet?" she asked her.

"Granny Nothing . . . this is the thirty-first of October."

Granny Nothing let out an ear-splitting shriek. A couple of street bulbs exploded. "I've got to get that Box shut before midnight! Stephanie, where's the key?"

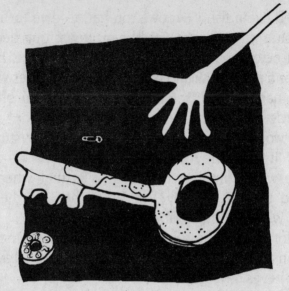

Chapter Twenty

The key was still at the bottom of my schoolbag – well, I didn't know it was all that important, did I? And I still didn't! Magic Box indeed! Containing the evils of the world? Honestly, what rubbish! There was a logical explanation for everything that had happened, including this blackout. Those mice had probably eaten through the electricity cables. But would anyone listen to me? Did anyone believe me? Of course not. This was much more exciting. Granny Nothing had them all racing about wildly. Polly was swinging her axe.

Todd Dangerfield was jumping up and down in excitement – either that or he desperately needed the toilet. Ewen was strangling me. "Where's the key? Where's the key?" he kept shouting.

I gave up. If you can't beat them, join them. "It's in my bag. I'll get it."

"Hurry up, Steph!" Granny Nothing shouted after me. "There's no' a minute to lose."

"Is this a race against time, Granny?" Polly screamed out.

"Aye, honey, it certainly is."

Polly grew even more excited. She swung her axe and it hit Todd so hard he almost swallowed his dummy. "Oh, I just love races against time!" she shouted.

They were all mad, I decided. Granny Nothing had made them that way.

When I came back with the key – held by a pair of rubber gloves, I might add, I wasn't touching that thing again – Granny Nothing snatched it from me and yelled, "Wagons Ho!"

Thomas roared like a wild animal, clinging on to her neck as she charged through the streets towards the carnival. Honestly, how does he stay attached to her? Does she use Velcro?

It was Hallowe'en, and yet the carnival was almost deserted. It was pathetic. The big dipper lay idle, the helter-skelter was boarded up and the hamburger stall had been closed by the town's health officer.

We found the Great Alfredo sitting dejectedly on the

steps of the hall of mirrors. He let out a big sigh when he saw Granny Nothing lumbering towards him. He waved around the place. "There's nothing left for you to break," he said, in a weedy voice. "My career is ruined. I'm just waiting for Mystico to finish his show and then I'm selling the carnival to him. Nothing else I can do."

Granny Nothing grabbed him by the collar and lifted him up. "Don't sell, Alfredo. I'm here to save your bacon."

He didn't look as if he believed her, and I didn't blame him.

"Right!" she said, setting him down again. "Where's this Mystico?"

Alfredo followed on behind us as we all hurried to Mystico's tent.

MYSTICO THE MAGNIFICENT, he was calling himself now. And his tent was crammed full of people, mostly our parents as far as I could see. There was Dad, dressed up as Batman with Mum as Robin. The Singhs, both dressed up as Elvis. Ha! Dressed up! They dressed like that every day.

Mystico was getting ready to do his final trick, with the help of the lovely Stew. She was standing beside him looking even more stupid than usual. It was as if the audience had been hypnotized. They couldn't take their eyes off Mystico as he produced silken scarves of blue and lilac and red and green from his sleeves and his pockets and his cloak. He blew softly in the air and a puff of yellow smoke surrounded the scarves and they disappeared and became fluttering budgies of blue and lilac and red and green.

"Boy, he's good," I muttered.

"He is now," Ewen said. "Look, there's the Box, Granny."

There it stood, at the back of the stage. It was still lying open and there seemed to be an eerie glow emanating from inside.

"I see it, son," Granny Nothing roared.

"See it, son," Thomas agreed, thwacking everyone on the head as Granny Nothing pushed her way through the crowd.

Mystico saw her coming. He could hardly miss a charging rhinoceros, could he? He gasped, and took a step back. "I command you to disappear!" he cried, throwing some kind of red dust all over her.

"Drap deid," she yelled. "I'm coming to get ye!"

"Drap deid," Thomas echoed. Granny Nothing lifted him from her neck and stuck him in my arms.

"Hold my boy!" she said, and then she was off again. Heading straight for Mystico.

"Stand behind me, Mystico my darling!" Nanny Sue stood in front of him to bar Granny Nothing's way.

"OK, Stew," Mystico said. Even at that romantic moment, when she was willing to give up her life – or at least a couple of limbs – for the man she loved, he couldn't get her name right.

Granny Nothing leapt on to the stage. She grabbed Nanny Sue by the leotard and dangled her in the air. Nanny Sue flailed about wildly.

Mystico was still trying to make Granny Nothing disappear.

"Eye of bat and an elephant's ear, I command you to disappear!"

A couple of budgies fell out of his cloak.

"By the power of Mystico, I command that you must go."

A fish popped out of his pocket.

The audience were going wild. They were sure this was all part of his act.

Granny Nothing dropped Nanny Sue into Dad's arms. "Keep a hold of her," she ordered. Then she turned back to Mystico. "Let me at that Box!" She was waving the Rusty Key about threateningly.

Mystico tried one last time.

"Wings of eagles, horns of moose, go! Be gone! Disappear! Vamoose!"

This time a tortoise appeared from his turban.

"The voodoo chief from Martinikee is protecting me," Granny Nothing told him.

At that news, Mystico shrieked. He didn't stand a chance and he knew it. Granny Nothing would have had him if it hadn't been for Nanny Sue. She screamed, struggling wildly in Dad's arms. He tried to hold her, but she was too strong for him.

Nanny Sue, the stick insect from hell, was too strong for him? Come on, Dad!

Nanny Sue seemed to fly from his arms. She threw herself at Granny Nothing just as she was reaching out to grab Mystico. Nanny Sue landed on Granny Nothing's shoulders. She clamped her hands round Granny Nothing's eyes. Her legs round her waist.

Ha! What waist. Anyway, whatever Nanny Sue's legs went round they hung on there like death.

And did Mystico save his beloved Stew? Did he billy-o! He was off, disappearing so fast I thought one of his vanishing spells had worked on him.

"Run, my beloved!" Nanny Sue shouted. "I'll catch up with you."

He didn't need telling twice. Mystico was gone.

It only took Granny Nothing a second to dislodge Nanny Sue, but it was that second that helped Mystico to make his escape. Granny Nothing flung open the curtains at the back of the stage but Mystico was nowhere to be seen.

At that very moment, the town clock began to chime midnight. It seemed to me the Box began to glow green. The ground beneath it began to shudder as if there was an earthquake coming. . .

Polly screamed. "Granny Nothing! Quick! Close the Box!"

But would she make it in time?

Chapter Twenty-one

Well, of course she made it in time – I only said that to make it more exciting. In fact, she made it with three chimes to go.

7 – she slammed the lid shut.

8 – she turned the key.

9 – the Box was locked.

Everyone gasped with relief. They clapped. They cheered. Granny Nothing turned round and took a bow.

I noticed that the Box wasn't glowing any more. It

was as if it was dead. It was, once more, just a box. A box . . . with a small b.

"Wow! That was a close thing!" Ewen said.

"What are you talking about, Ewen? She closed a box. That was it. Look at it. It's only a box."

He looked at me as if I was the one who was mad. "Honestly, Steph, you are so thick."

Me? Thick? That's a laugh. But in a way I knew Ewen was right. I felt as if I had been awoken from a spell myself. Mystico and his hypnotic eyes were gone. The spell was broken. It was just a box. That was all it had ever been.

Granny Nothing took the Rusty Key and dropped it down the front of her dress. "There ye are, I'd like to see anybody try to get it now."

It would be a brave man indeed who'd go down there for that key. She rubbed her hands together. "Well, that's that. Now, back to the house for my finger buffet."

Suddenly, Nanny Sue leapt on to the stage again. "Where is my beloved Mystico? What have you done with him?" She didn't wait for an answer. She was off and out of the back of the tent, running like a headless chicken.

"Thank heaven that's sorted," Dad said, and all at once I saw that Mum was almost crying.

"No thanks to you! You can't do anything right. You couldn't even hold on to Nanny Sue."

Dad was crestfallen. I have never seen a crest so fallen in my life. His cheeks were red and his head hung in shame. "Sorry," he mumbled.

Ewen was full of sympathy. "It wasn't his fault, Mum." He turned to me. "It wasn't, Steph."

"Don't look at me," I said. "I'm on Mum's side. He is useless."

I was definitely with Mum on this one.

Ewen looked up at Granny Nothing. "Do something, Granny."

Granny Nothing's warts were twinkling thoughtfully. Then she winked at Ewen. "Leave it to me," she whispered.

It was right at that moment Mrs Singh screamed. At first I thought she was launching herself into another Elvis number. Instead she yelled, "Where's my Elvis!" She was looking all around her in a panic.

Presley let out a howl. He was looking for him too. Now, you never saw Presley without Elvis, or Elvis without Presley. I was beginning to get worried too. Presley let out another howl and his turban wobbled.

Mrs Singh was frantic. "Where can he be?"

Granny Nothing's face was suddenly serious. She thumped off the stage. "Oh . . . I forgot about this, Steph." Her voice was a whisper. "When the box is closed, it always takes somebody with it."

"You mean he's inside the box? Open it then."

I was almost down the front of her dress for the key.

"No, not inside the box. When the box is closed, someone disappears, never to be seen again."

Ewen turned chalk white. "You mean, Elvis?"

"I hope I'm wrong." She shouted out to everyone:

"Let's spread out, and look for the boy." And then she mumbled. "And let's hope we find him."

Everyone left the tent, calling out Elvis's name, searching for him in tents, in caravans, in bushes. We looked in the hall of mirrors. He wasn't there. The fat lady hadn't seen him. The bearded lady hadn't seen him.

Alfredo sat down on the steps of the ghost train. He let out a howl like Presley's. "I can see the headline now. 'Child goes missing at carnival'. I'll be run out of town."

Granny Nothing lifted him to his feet. "The only thing that matters now is finding Elvis."

Alfredo joined us, calling Elvis's name. Mrs Singh was crying. Mr Singh was trying not to. Mum had her arms around them. She was crying too. "We'll find him, Mrs Singh."

But I was beginning to worry. What if we couldn't find him? What if he really had been taken by the box? I was so worried I was almost ready to believe all the rubbish. That the box did have magic powers that had been unleashed when I opened it with the Rusty Key.

Baldy was following us about with his banner. "I told everyone something like this would happen. Why doesn't anyone listen to me?"

No one listened to him.

We had searched everywhere, almost given up, when we heard a faint cry. The unmistakable voice of Elvis. "Help!"

We looked all around. We listened again.

"It's coming from the sky," Ewen said, his voice was full of awe. "It's a voice from heaven."

We all looked up to the stars.

But Elvis wasn't calling from heaven. He was perched in a car, right at the top of the big dipper.

Chapter Twenty-two

Mrs Singh took one look and fainted. Mr Singh fell to his knees to try to revive her. Presley let out a wail and he tried to climb the big dipper.

"Help!" Elvis shouted again.

Now that I knew where he was I was beginning to get annoyed at him. "How did you get up there! You could have been hurt. I'll kill you when you come down here."

Granny Nothing pushed up her sleeves. "I'm coming, Elvis," she roared and she lifted Thomas from her neck – what neck! – and handed him to Mum. "Hold my boy!"

"You'll be all right now, Elvis!" Ewen shouted up to him. "Granny Nothing's coming to get you."

This time a promise, not a threat.

"Oh, this takes me back to my days as a steeplejack in New York, in the US of A."

Ewen's mouth fell open. "A steeplejack? Isn't that a horse?"

That boy is so thick it's embarrassing. "That's a steeplechaser. A steeplejack's someone who builds skyscrapers."

Granny Nothing tucked her skirt into her big pink silk knickers. Then she began to climb.

"Oh well, as usual it's your mother to the rescue." It was my mum, and her words were directed at Dad.

Right at that moment there was a cry from Granny Nothing; a cry of pain. She clutched at her heart with one hand and started swaying dangerously. Everyone screamed.

She let out a roar and then she fell to the ground with such a thud the crowd bounced in the air. It was just like the last scene from *King Kong* when the great ape tumbles from the top of the Empire State Building.

I ran to her. "Granny Nothing! What's wrong?"

"It's my dicky ticker. I'll never be able to climb now."

"Your Dicky Ticker?" Ewen asked puzzled. "Is that one of your old boyfriends?"

"It's her heart, stupid!" I told him. Granny Nothing

had a weak heart? Oh no. There couldn't be anything weak about Granny Nothing.

Mr Singh dropped his wife's head and it hit the ground with a crack and she passed out again. "I'll go up!" he cried.

Granny Nothing grabbed him by the cloak. "No, Mr Singh, you'll never be able to climb in them Elvis Presley silk trousers. No . . . we need somebody else." She paused dramatically. "Preferably somebody young and fit and related to me," she said.

I was astonished. "You want *me* to go up there?"

She gave me such a look. "No, not you. I mean somebody else." She was pointing her warts in one direction. All at once, I knew who that somebody else was. Dad. I looked straight at him. So did Ewen. Even Thomas was staring at him.

Dad looked behind him, then back at us. He pointed a finger at his chest. "Me?" He swallowed. "You don't mean . . . me?" Now he sounded astonished.

"You're my son. Of course I mean you!"

Dad looked up at Elvis, who was peering over the edge of the car. "Help!" he shouted again.

"But I don't like heights," Dad said.

Granny Nothing was quick to reassure him. "Don't worry about that, son. If you fall, you can land on me."

He looked at Mum. He knew he had to do something to restore her faith in him. He looked back up at Elvis and bit his lip. "Right. I'll do it," he said.

The whole dipper shuddered as he started to climb. I think it was because Dad was shaking with terror.

109

Up he went, one shaky step at a time, his Batman cloak flying out behind him. Some wit in the crowd started to hum the Batman theme. I'm sure everyone would have joined in, if just at that moment his foot hadn't slipped. It dangled in mid-air. Everyone watching from below screamed as he struggled for a foothold.

"You can do it, son!" Granny Nothing yelled up to him, and Dad began climbing again.

Up and up he went while everyone below held their collective breath.

At last he was there. He reached Elvis and gave us all a victory wave. The crowd cheered and applauded. I was really quite proud of him. So was Granny Nothing. "That's my boy!" she said.

Mum had tears in her eyes. "My hero!" she called up to him.

We were all watching closely. Dad was in the car now with Elvis and we waited expectantly for them both to climb down.

And waited.

And waited.

Finally, they waved and both of them called down to us. "Help!" they squeaked.

"I don't believe it!" I said.

Mum ran to Granny Nothing. "You've got to do something. He's been brave enough for one day!"

"You're sure?"

Mum sniffed away a tear and nodded. "I'm sure."

Granny Nothing got to her feet and brushed herself

down. "Oh well, I suppose I'd better go up there for the two of them," she said.

"What about your dicky ticker?" Ewen asked her, though I'm sure he still thought it was an old boyfriend.

"Me? I've got a heart like an ox!" Granny Nothing told him.

"You mean, you pretended you were ill just so Dad would go up there?" I asked.

She bent down and whispered. "Well, I couldn't have everybody thinking my boy was useless . . . especially your mum."

And as we watched her climb up like a monkey, with her skirt still tucked into her knickers, I couldn't stop thinking that was the kindest thing she had ever done!

Chapter Twenty-three

So Granny Nothing brought them both down in a fireman's lift. As soon as they reached the ground Elvis was covered in kisses by his mum and dad, and Presley was licking his face. Dad was being covered in kisses too . . . by Mum.

"That's disgusting!" Ewen said. "In front of children too."

That was when Nanny Sue appeared again. I thought we'd seen the last of her. "What have you done with my darling Mystico?" she screamed at Granny Nothing. "I can't find him anywhere. He's disappeared off the face of the earth."

Ewen gasped. Granny Nothing shook her head. "I see what's happened now. The box had to take somebody. It wasn't Elvis, so it must have been your Mystico."

"The box took him," Ewen said in wonder, and Granny Nothing nodded.

"Wouldn't you disappear off the face of the earth if Nanny Sue wanted to marry you?" I suggested.

Nanny Sue whipped out her notebook. "This is going into my portfolio," she said. "You have lost me the only man I will ever love."

"Aw, shut your gob!" Granny Nothing said, and Thomas echoed his agreement: "Shut your gob."

Baldy was running about wildly waving his banner. "I told you no good would come of this carnival. Now, will someone listen to me!"

No one listened to him.

"It doesn't matter now anyway." The Great Alfredo was almost in tears. "I'll have to close down the carnival. Mystico was the only act making any money and now he's gone. I'll just have to accept it. My carnival's rubbish."

No one disagreed with him there. But you couldn't help feeling sorry for the little soul. It was Granny Nothing who came to the rescue . . . as usual.

"You will not close down your carnival, Alfredo. Because we are all going to help you bring in the crowds."

He looked at her as if she was mad . . . which of course, she is.

"And how are you going to do that?" he asked.

Granny Nothing looked around everyone gathered there. "This is a talented bunch we've got here, don't you know that?"

It was the first I had heard it. Us, a talented bunch? The Elvis Lookalike Singhs? My dad in his Batman outfit with his tights all torn? Ridiculous maybe, talented, never. She must be joking.

She wasn't.

"We are all going to use our talents and give you. . ." At this she bellowed like an elephant ". . .the Greatest Show on Earth."

The November sun shone crisp and bright on the day of the Greatest Show on Earth. Granny Nothing had bribed or coaxed or threatened everyone to take part. Half the town turned up just to see the fun. Even if we were all rubbish, and there was no doubt we would be, they knew they at least would have a laugh.

Alfredo couldn't stop thanking everyone. "My friends," he said over and over. "I will be grateful for all eternity for what you are doing for me. But I too will do my bit. I will have a surprise for you all before this day is over."

Baldy was still protesting, marching up and down with his banner and shouting. "What do we want?

The carnival to go!

When do we want it to go?

Now!

As usual, nobody listened to him.

Everyone had a part to play. Mrs Scoular had decided to tell fortunes. She turned up draped from head to toe in multicoloured scarves. Mrs Singh had provided most of them. You couldn't see her face. Not a bad thing, really. She said she wanted to look like a Hungarian gypsy.

"Do you think she looks Hungarian?" Ewen asked me.

I didn't even think she looked human.

And she nearly caused a riot. She told everybody they would be dead in six months.

"You're reading the tea leaves upside down, hen," Granny Nothing told her. "Tell them they're all going to have babies and win the lottery."

Nanny Sue was selling kisses. Or she was trying to. The only one who was waiting at her stall was the man who kept picking his nose in the dark. It was great fun watching her trying to fend him off.

Mr and Mrs Singh naturally did their famous Elvis Presley impersonations. They sang duets, if singing is the right word for the noise they made. They sang solo. They were so delighted that their tent was packed to capacity.

"Maybe we should do this for a living, my dear," Mr Singh said during one of their breaks.

No one had the heart to tell him that Ewen and I were making a fortune selling earplugs of the reinforced variety, or that Granny Nothing was giving a prize to the person who could stay in their tent the longest.

Dad had decided he'd be the tightrope walker. "After climbing up the big dipper I've completely lost my fear of heights!" he said. "I can do anything."

"He is good," Ewen said, totally impressed.

You wonder why I think my brother is daft?

Dad's tightrope was three feet off the ground – and he had a safety net – and he kept falling off anyway!

Mum, his beautiful assistant, would run to him after each fall and cover him with kisses. "My hero!" she would say.

Honestly, my whole family is completely loopy. I'm the only sensible one there is.

Polly was running about looking for someone she could saw in half. We all suggested Nanny Sue.

Todd Dangerfield got in on the act too. We made him sit on a swing balanced above a tank of water, and you could throw coconuts at him – if you hit the target, he went right into the tank. Todd had bullied so many people that the whole school lined up to get back at him.

"This isn't fair!" he kept saying every time he emerged dripping to get back on the swing. "I'm trying to turn over a new leaf."

Elvis was the bare-back rider. Since he didn't have a horse, he rode Presley who bucked and whinnied very authentically.

"That dog should be an actor," everyone said.

Presley seemed to hear and understand. He stood

on his hind legs and started dancing. He was just showing off, if you ask me. Elvis was thrown to the ground, but like a true trouper he was on his feet in an instant and started singing: "A four-legged friend."

They were a great attraction. "Bollywood, here we come!" Elvis shouted.

Granny Nothing was the World's Strongest Woman.

She balanced at least four people over her head. She lifted the fat lady with one hand. I was so embarrassed I tore a telephone book in half.

DID YOU HEAR WHAT I JUST SAID?
I TORE A TELEPHONE BOOK IN HALF!!!

No. It must have been a skinny little tiny telephone book. I am not like Granny Nothing. I am neat and petite and sweet and feminine. . .

And I can tear telephone books in half.

I give up.

Granny Nothing was in the middle of taking her third bow when suddenly a gorilla burst from one of the tents, pounding his chest and roaring like a . . . well, like a gorilla really. He rushed into the crowd.

"It's Alfredo," Granny Nothing said. "Don't hurt his feelings. Kid on you're frightened."

We duly did as we were told. We started to scream and run about as if our lives depended on it. The gorilla ran about too, dragging his great arms along the ground.

"That costume's good, isn't it?" Ewen whispered

between screams. And I had to admit he was right. This one fitted better and it was much more authentic-looking.

Suddenly, there was another roar. This time from Baldy. "This is what I mean about frightening children with your pathetic disguise, Alfredo! Well, I won't stand for it. I am coming to get you."

And he did. He ran straight at the gorilla. "Right you! Back in the cage. See how you like being locked up." He tried to lift the gorilla, but instead the gorilla lifted him. I didn't think little Alfredo had it in him.

"Alfredo! Put me down!" Baldy tried to put him in a neck-hold. He didn't manage it. Alfredo lifted him even higher and waggled him about like a rag doll. Everyone applauded. "Wonderful, Alfredo," they shouted.

"I'm getting angry now, Alfredo! And you won't like me when I'm angry." Baldy grabbed the gorilla's head and tried to yank it off. He pulled and he tugged, but nothing happened. The gorilla just began to look annoyed. Baldy tugged again. Still nothing.

"Alfredo, I know you're in there. Come out and fight like a man!" Baldy screamed into the gorilla's ear as he was shaken about. "Alfredo! Are you in there?"

"No, actually I'm over here," a weedy little voice called from the back of the crowd. The unmistakable weedy little voice of Alfredo.

We all turned to stare at him. Then we all looked back at Baldy, held high in the air. He stared at Alfredo. Then he looked back at the gorilla.

"I see you've met Gordon already," Alfredo said happily. "That was my surprise."

Baldy let out a strangled shriek . . . and then he fainted.

Chapter Twenty-four

Everyone began to panic when they realized the gorilla was a real gorilla, and not Alfredo in a monkey suit. Gordon still held Baldy's limp body in the air with one paw. He pummelled his chest with the other. Then he roared. He roared so loud he blew Alfredo off his feet.

"Oh dear, I think he's annoyed," Alfredo said.

"What are we going to do?" someone shouted. "Who's going to save Baldy?"

Who else?

Granny Nothing swung Thomas from her shoulders.

"Hold my boy," she said, handing him to me. "I'll handle this."

"Don't tell me," I said drily. "You used to train gorillas when you lived in the Congo."

She let out one of her belly laughs, and with her belly that was some laugh. "Me? Not at all. But I used to be a bouncer in a club in Glasgow. Handling a gorilla's nothing once you've lived there."

She pounded towards Gordon.

"Drop Baldy, Gordon," she ordered, "and step back from the teacher."

Gordon turned a beady eye on her. He shook poor old Baldy about a bit more and then he roared again.

Granny Nothing roared back and Gordon almost fell over. He pounded his chest. She pounded hers.

Gordon stamped his feet in anger.

Granny Nothing stamped hers and the earth shuddered.

Everyone was holding their breath. You could have heard a pin drop – or even a very skinny teacher like Baldy. And that was the only sound we did hear as Gordon dropped him to the ground.

Gordon charged at Granny Nothing. She charged at him. They were locked together like a couple of sumo wrestlers. It was a brilliant spectacle.

But it was no contest really. One minute they were tackling each other and the next, Granny Nothing had Gordon in an arm-lock and was dragging him back to his cage. He looked like one terrified gorilla.

"Now, you get in there, Gordon." Granny Nothing

dropped him on the floor and closed the cage door. "It won't be for long, I promise. We're not keeping a lovely boy like you caged up."

Gordon sat down with his mouth open. He looked gobsmacked. Can gorillas look gobsmacked? Gordon certainly did.

"OK? I've got to see to Baldy now," she said to him. Gordon nodded as if he understood.

Granny Nothing lumbered over to the limp, lifeless body of Baldy. (Here, that was quite poetic, wasn't it? The limp, lifeless, body of Baldy.)

"Is he dead?" Polly shouted, hopefully.

"No. I think he's just fainted," Ewen sounded disappointed.

"Leave this to me." Granny Nothing knelt beside him and lifted his head in her arms. "Good thing I did that stint with the Red Cross. Took a first-aid course. Stand back, I'm going to give him the kiss of life."

And she did. In fact, for a minute there I thought she'd swallowed him. His head seemed to disappear into her mouth.

Everyone looked sick. Some couldn't bear to look and had to turn away.

"He's going to need the kiss of life to recover from the kiss of life," I murmured to my brother.

However, it worked. Granny Nothing sat back on her heels and Baldy began to stir. He opened his eyes and looked around us all. "What happened ?" he asked. "I dreamt I was being swallowed by a rhinoceros."

Granny Nothing roared with laughter. "Not at all,

Baldy, that was me. I was giving you the kiss of life."

Baldy looked at her in horror. Then he fainted again.

So, the carnival was saved. Granny Nothing gave the bearded lady a few tips on how to grow a proper beard and the Great Alfredo and Gordon the gorilla rolled off into the sunset. On one condition, Granny Nothing said: Gordon was never again to be put into a cage. So instead, Alfredo gave him his caravan, and Alfredo went into the cage. It seemed a much better idea somehow.

"I'll miss that wee man," Granny Nothing said.

"I bet he won't miss you,"I told her.

And we never saw Mystico again.

"The box took him." Ewen was convinced about that.

"He probably just joined another carnival."

Nanny Sue said she would never forgive Granny Nothing for losing her the love of her life.

"I swear vengeance," she told us one day. "That woman . . . if she is a woman, has a secret, and one day I will find out what it is."

I had a feeling she meant it.

We were so fed up with listening to her that we all helped Presley bury her in the garden.

And Dad finally finished his "conservative". I just hope it doesn't collapse on us.

He threw a party to celebrate. Everyone was invited. The Singhs were there, and Mrs Scoular. Even Baldy dared to come, though I noticed he kept well away from Granny Nothing. I don't think he's quite recovered from the kiss of life. He's had counselling ever since.

When everyone was gathered together, Dad opened a bottle of red wine and poured his guests a drink.

"You know," Granny Nothing said as they sipped, "this takes me back to my days tramping grapes in the Dordogne." (She pronounced it Dor-dog-ney.) "You know, tramping them grapes was the only thing that ever helped my feet."

I could see everyone trying not to swallow their wine. They didn't manage it.

"I never had any trouble with my corns or my verrucas when I was tramping them grapes." She sighed. "Happy days." She held up her glass and looked around. "What's wrong with your faces? You look as if you've seen a ghost. Drink up!" She lifted her glass triumphantly. "Who knows? This might be the very wine I tramped with my very own feet."

Stranger things have happened . . . and with Granny Nothing around, they usually do.